The Tailor of Bridewater Bay

A novel by

C.R. Fagan

BLUE
CEDAR
PRESS

Wichita, Kansas

Blue Cedar Press
PO Box 48715
Wichita, KS 67201

Visit the Blue Cedar Press website: www.bluecedarpress.com
10 9 8 7 6 5 4 3 2 1 First edition

ISBN: 978-1-958728-38-3 (paper)
ISBN: 978-1-958728-39-0 (ebook)

Cover Art: Duck Land
Interior Design: Gina Laiso, Integrita Productions
Editors: Laura Tillem and Gretchen Eick
Library of Congress Control Number: LCCN: 2025938706

Printed in the United States of America

Dedication:

For my partner,
the easiest part of this book to write
was the hummingbird that flew
from my chest to Rónán's.

Prologue: September 1877

Aislyn sucked air in quickly between her teeth in a gasp of pain. A bright crimson drop emerged from the calloused skin at the tip of her long, slender finger. She pulled her finger to her mouth, tasting warm, metallic blood. Shaking the sharp pain from her finger, Aislyn looked down to see the culprit: a stray sewing needle left in the fold of an embroidered blanket. In her nearly thirty years of sewing, she had pricked herself more times than she could count—the rough skin on her fingers was proof enough of that—but the hidden needle spoke to the unintentional carelessness of youth. She made a mental note to remind her son to be more careful when he was cleaning up. She picked up the blanket with her uninjured hand to avoid leaving red marks on the white fabric and tucked it into her wicker basket between the vials of her home-brewed medicine. With the basket in the crook of her arm, she set off out the front door.

The beat of Aislyn's soles against the groaning boardwalk of Bridewater Bay added a percussive pulse to her soft humming. The syncopated tinkle of cotton and glass sounding from the basket bouncing against her hip joined the chorus of her humming. Aislyn walked along the bay-facing path, made old by decades of sun and seawater, along the storefronts of Bridewater. Every few feet, a shop awning provided her with a shadowed respite from the sun. She squinted into the bright daylight and brushed a bead of sweat from her temple. It was unseasonably hot and humid for a late September afternoon, even on the Louisiana coast, and the air clung to her skin like an unwanted hug. Most days, Rónán, her copper-headed son who could have been her twin down to the last sun-kissed freckle, was more than eager to make the deliveries, but today, Aislyn had more than just deliveries to attend to.

As Aislyn walked toward the general store and the sick child who waited for her there, she considered the town around her—this community nestled between the gulf and miles of briny bayou. Bridewater was neither all that beautiful, as tendrils of swampland had crept in over the years, nor all that welcoming, but it was the place where her husband had died and a month later, her son was born. Sometimes she felt tied to this place by the memories. Other times, she thought about leaving, returning with her son to her girlhood home in Ireland. But by the time her letter containing the news of her husband's death crossed the Atlantic, and her mother's words returned, Aislyn felt stuck, like a boot suctioned into thick mud.

With her free hand, Aislyn traced the cracked edges of sun-bleached paint on the storefront windows as she strolled along the row of shops. Looking to her left, she could just make out the silhouette of an old wooden ship on the horizon. Like Bridewater, it hadn't modernized, unlike the steam ships that chugged farther out in the salty waters on their way to New Orleans. The sight of the old ship sent a dull ache through her chest, reminding her of the anniversary this late spring day marked. She shook her head, trying to free herself from the memory. There was too much to face today without the creeping sadness that sometimes threatened to drown her now.

"Afternoon, ma'am."

The voice of the elder Mr. Francis brought her back from her reverie. The dock owner tipped his hat at Aislyn, and she nodded with her bonnet.

"Hello," she returned. Her lilting Irish accent painted the air between them. "How is Mrs. Francis?"

"Much better since you visited," he said. "Her cough is nearly gone. I can't thank you enough."

Recently, Aislyn found herself busy making house calls in addition to her usual deliveries from the tailor shop, bringing her neighbors tinctures made from spotted weeds, stinging nettles, and black willow leaves foraged from the surrounding wetlands. A sudden flu, suspected of being cargo on one of the ships that anchored in the bay, had gripped Bridewater in hacking coughs and aching heads.

"I am glad to hear it," Aislyn smiled.

Mr. Francis scratched the top of his head for a moment, as if trying to dig out what to say next. "It's terrible what happened to the baker's boy," he said.

As the flu's grip tightened on the small town, the sickness had claimed the souls of several of Bridewater's own. Just last week, Polter, the baker's son, who was around Rónán's age, passed in the night as he struggled to breathe.

"And old Mrs. Parker," Mr. Francis continued, "Her son found her dead in front of the fireplace—her bible still open in her lap to Revelations."

Aislyn shuddered thinking of those recent deaths. If she only had the time and the supplies, she would visit every home in Bridewater, protecting the souls of the young and old alike, but, unfortunately for her and her neighbors, that was not possible.

"Her funeral is next week at the old Presbyterian," Mr. Francis said, nodding toward the steeple that lay out of sight behind her. "We'd love to see you there."

Aislyn didn't say anything. Even after all their years in Bridewater, Aislyn and Rónán were likely the only two townsfolk who did not appreciate the fire and brimstone at the white-steepled church. Something about the building's presence always made Aislyn slightly uncomfortable. It stood out like a statue on a plinth, always painted freshly white, somehow the only building in Bridewater freed from the defects of time and decay. The empty windows along the front of the church were like eyes that burrowed into her no matter where she went in town.

"I appreciate you letting me know," Aislyn finally said. "I'm glad to hear your wife is doing better, but I have to go now." She gestured to her basket, showing him the contents, hoping he understood. He nodded politely, and she continued her walk toward the general store.

As usual, Aislyn found this interaction with Mr. Francis somewhat odd. She didn't necessarily think of herself and her son as outcasts, but every interaction with her neighbors dripped with a distinctly saccharine veneer of southern charm. Aislyn and Rónán were kept at a polite distance, like the stray cats that wandered in the alley between the two rows of shops in town, being fed table scraps at the back door, but only invited inside when help was needed to catch a mouse. When Aislyn's prowess in tailoring or her skills in home medicine were required, everyone treated them like close friends. Then, like in every other small town, as soon as she was out of earshot, her secrets were whispered behind some housewife's palm.

Aislyn rounded the corner and padded toward the general store, which served as a sort of catch-all for the people of Bridewater—chemist, confectioner, and grocer. With the hand not cradling her basket of goods, Aislyn reached up, tucking a stray piece of her scarlet hair back under the linen bonnet knotted under her chin. The aging piece of cloth was one of the few items besides her violin that she brought with her from Ireland. It was also one of the first pieces of clothing she made under the direction of her own mother's lessons, which were as much lessons of family history as they were of sewing skills. She couldn't count the number of times she pricked her thumb while learning her family craft, gasping and pulling blood-soaked threads through scrap fabric while sitting at her mother's feet. The Ogham stitches lining the seams of her bonnet—somewhere between ornamental embroidery and secure fastening—were laced with her mother's Druidic prayers of protection, health, and love.

As her finger brushed against the fabric of her bonnet, Aislyn was flooded by another memory. She was, of course, thankful for her mother's gifts, but like most things good, they didn't come without their own cost. She had learned to read the Ogham patterns in her stitches, divining glimpses of her future in the hatched lines of threads, and, around nine years ago, she saw something that made her want to tie a knot in her craft altogether. Just hours after giving birth to her boy, she saw her own death foretold, embedded in the folds of fabric that lined her bed. She didn't know exactly when or how—her gift could not tell her that. Divining through the fabric was like trying to cross an unfamiliar room after midnight. You knew what should be waiting in front of you, but the darkness obscured the shapes. Aislyn would stretch her hands into that darkness and feel for the familiar, but something shrouded would cause her to stumble. What she grasped that day on her birthing bed was that she would someday leave her son behind. But today, she couldn't think about that. Today, she was caring for another child.

Aislyn pushed the door to the general store open and the soft chime of the bell hanging above the door announced her arrival. The general store lay in out-of-character disarray, even for a low traffic town like Bridewater. Emptiness lined the shelves where rows of produce and product used to sit. It reminded her of a time when an intense storm moved through the bay. As the clouds churned overhead and the bay seethed below, people in town flocked to the general store clearing it of all foods, oils, and matches—those too slow to stock up be damned. "Hello," Aislyn called out into the empty room in her melodic voice.

The tan face of Henriette Hebert, the shopkeeper's wife, rounded the corner of a hallway leading to a cluster of back rooms. Tall, slender Mrs. Hebert was beautiful. Her high cheekbones, wide almond eyes, and dark curls gave her an air of elegant austerity, like a strict schoolmaster who also kept sweets in her desk. Aislyn knew Henriette and her husband to be generally warm and kind people, but she could sense the exhaustion in Henriette's movements. Henriette feigned a pleasant smile, but worry was pressed into every crease of her cinnamon-colored face. A plum shadow blossomed under her reddened eyes, a sign that the woman had been crying and likely not sleeping. Aislyn gave her a warm smile. The lines in Henriette's face seemed to ease ever-so-slightly, but the edge of worry stayed suspended on her face like a fog creeping through the bayou.

"Helene is in the back," Henriette said quietly in her southern accent. "I've been trying to keep her warm—damn this heat—but she cannot shake the chill."

Henriette motioned for Aislyn to follow and led her to a small room at the back of the store. Pushed into a back corner of the room sat a heavy oaken desk littered with papers, catalogs, and dried rings of coffee. This room must've usually served as Mr. Hebert's office, but positioned in the middle of the floor was a child-sized bed.

"She was too exhausted to continue taking the stairs," Henriette said, catching Aislyn's wandering eyes. Nodding toward the back of the room, she continued, "And we thought it would be good for her to stay near the fire."

Aislyn looked toward portly Mr. Hebert who stood at the back of the room, alternately stoking the flames in the fireplace and looking out the small window. Though he had always been fairly rotund, his dark skin was painted with a bloodless pink hue and shiny sweat. He reflected his store—unusually unkempt. His sleeves were rolled to his elbows, the top buttons of his shirt remained unfastened, and a strip of shiny, black fabric, usually tied into a bowtie, hung limp around his thick neck. With a nervous tick, he passed his unoccupied hand over his thick, curly black hair as if to straighten it, but if he were ashamed for Aislyn to see him in this state, he didn't show it. His face, like his wife's, only reflected worry for his little girl.

Hector nodded a solemn greeting at Aislyn, which she took as permission to approach the girl. With a soft clink, Aislyn placed her wicker basket on the ground next to the girl's bed. She looked down at Helene, who was only a year younger than her own Rónán. Dense sweat slicked the curly hairs near the girl's hairline to her forehead and left reflective trails down her mottled face. Helene's eyelids were slightly parted, like a child trying to sneakily catch a glimpse of where her friends had run to hide during a game of hide-and-seek, and she was breathing heavily, as if she just finished chasing another child. Placing her palm flat on the girl's forehead, Aislyn could feel the clammy, cold sickness burning through her skin. Aislyn leaned an ear toward her mouth. A slight, shaking rattle sounded in each labored breath the girl took. The muscles beneath her ribcage rose and fell in uneven movements, working hard to bring the warm, salty air of the office into her lungs.

Aislyn reached into her basket and retrieved a small glass bottle. A murky, greenish liquid sloshed around inside. She handed this homemade, natural tincture to Henriette, but addressed both adults at the same time.

"Give her a spoonful every morning and every evening," Aislyn instructed. "This will help with any pain and restlessness." She eyed the fireplace next to Hector and continued, "And put that fire out. This fever is not meant to be sweated out."

The couple acknowledged that they understood, without saying a word. They shared a glance with one another, and, whether by fear or awe, they just sat back and watched the woman work. Like when she was sewing, Aislyn entered a certain mode when her brain was occupied with healing. Her focus turned back to the girl, and she pulled the thick, heavy quilt off Helene, releasing the cloud of heat that was trapped beneath. Aislyn reached into her basket. With a small flourish, she pulled out the embroidered blanket she brought from home, unfolding it with a flick of her wrists. Tenderly, she placed it on top of the sick girl's body, spreading it neatly over the bed. The white cloth was embroidered with a spiraling field of flowers in a shade of violet so light, the flora was nearly imperceptible. The spiraling peonies were shaped from neat, tight stitches of Ogham, placed perfectly together. She had stayed up two nights in a row, working by flickering candlelight and steady moonlight, carefully sewing each blossom into the cloth as she incanted her own charms of health into the fabric.

She placed her left hand on Helene's chest and leaned in close to the child, as if she were trying to kiss her on the forehead. Then, she breathed something in a soft, melodic whisper. The girl's parents leaned towards Aislyn to try to hear—to understand—but they couldn't make out the words. Even if they could hear Aislyn clearly, the shopkeeper and his wife were not sure they would understand. The syllables sounded foreign to their ears. Aislyn, with her mouth still hovering above the girl's head, muttered another prayer, another incantation she learned from her mother. Then, as her song of prayer ended, she lightly kissed the child's forehead and brushed her thumb across her brow.

Unsure if they noticed a change or just wished so hard for one that they imagined it, both Heberts sighed guttural and shaky exhalations as if they had been holding their breath. Aislyn knew the bottle she brought meant comfort for the girl and for her parents, but she also knew that if this girl recovered, it was not from some boiled leaves bottled together. Instead, it was Aislyn's mother's blessing. It was the charm delicately stitched in Ogham into the field of purple flowers. It was the intention of Aislyn and the will of her ancestors who passed this family gift from mother to child from time immemorial. Already the little girl seemed to breathe easier.

Aislyn stood.

"Madame, I thank you for coming," Hector said in his Creole accent through the bristles of his walrus-like mustache. "Please," he continued, "take this."

The shopkeeper reached above the mantle of the fireplace, which held only a few glowing embers. He brought down a small burlap sack just bigger than his fist. He handed the rough bag to Aislyn, who tucked it into her basket. The soft crinkling she heard as she grasped the bag hinted at the various candies inside. She suspected this gift was the Heberts' way of recognizing her own child, who loved the cherry discs Hector gave him in trade for every delivery. Though of course she was paid for much of her work, the people of Bridewater, Aislyn included, were not opposed to trading. It was what they did to get by. Aislyn accepted with a smile any offering that was given in good faith for her services.

With a polite nod to the parents, Aislyn picked up her basket and saw herself out of the shop, the bell announcing her departure. Stepping into the golden afternoon sun, Aislyn lifted her face and breathed deeply through her nose, her shoulders rising and falling in exaggerated movements. Then, resuming her song, she began humming to herself as she made the remaining deliveries of the day along the boardwalk of Bridewater Bay.

When Aislyn returned to the tailor shop, she found her son, Rónán, sitting on the floor practicing his stitches. Sprawled in front of him was a tanned leather-bound notebook with handwritten notes and an Ogham chart Rónán had drawn himself. Each family or aicme *of the alphabet—Beithe, Huatha, Muine, and* Ailme— *contained different characters. And the hatched, parallel, slanted, and crossed lines that made up the alphabet were the vessels that allowed the family magic to bloom. Aislyn had taught Rónán how to stitch them and had begun showing him how to divine the secrets they contained, but he was still learning.*

Aislyn looked down at her boy in admiration and wonder. She could lace, embroider, craft, and create, but how she could birth something so beautiful, she would never know. His red hair, his freckles, and his milky white skin, were all from her. But his green eyes, as verdant as the sunlight through a treetop canopy, were a gift from his father. The pang in her heart over her husband's death stung less than it had a decade ago, but she would never stop longing for him. She ached that her husband and son, the two people in her life who represented so much love, never got to meet. A radiating warmth overtook her as she watched her young son. He too might be out of place in Bridewater, but at least they were out of place together.

Aislyn padded behind the counter, a long wooden surface that doubled as a place of greeting and a worktable. Bending down, she placed her basket below the till. She picked up another project she was working on, a set of small handkerchiefs for one of the older women in town.

"Come," she said, gesturing for Rónán to follow her.

As they sat together in front of the shop, Aislyn in her rocking chair and Rónán on the bare planks of the boardwalk, they worked— Aislyn hemming her charms into the woman's handkerchiefs and Rónán practicing his lessons. Aislyn taught her son the same way she learned from her own mother: through story, through song, and through practice. Every now and then, she would pause to fold the napkins in her lap and lean toward her son. Scanning his project, she would offer guidance, fixing a line here or angling a stitch differently there.

Even at his young age, Rónán was skilled enough now in the technical side of sewing that he would often help her with the various jobs in her shop, something that both impressed the neighbors and invited their whispers. Most young men in town worked at the docks, so seeing the boy toiling away on a gown in the tailor shop was a bit of an oddity. Though Bridewater was small, they managed to keep a steady enough flow of work and kept themselves afloat in the absence of her husband. Of course, Aislyn ran the only tailor shop in town, so people came to her for even the smallest of projects that any good homemaker knew, or at least should know, how to do. What they did not know, and what would probably incite more than just whispers, was that Aislyn stitched her magic into every seam, something Rónán still needed practice doing.

Though her neighbors remained unaware, she knew some part of them felt the rewards.

As the sun faded from the gold of the evening to the purple of twilight, a light breeze from over the bay finally provided some respite from the oppressive heat. It was still hot, yes, but she appreciated the intermittent cool. Aislyn set her work aside and looked down to see her son rubbing his eyes.

"Time for sleep, little seal," she laughed, as the boy stretched with a gaping yawn.

Aislyn had begun pulling the curtains of the front window of the shop to signal they were closed when she heard a faint, papery rustling behind her. She turned in time to see her son bring his hand up to his mouth with a sly smirk and a barely contained giggle.

"Rónán," she said, furrowing her brow in a look of mock disapproval.

Rónán laughed, sending the freckles on his cheeks dancing. Through the fresh gap in his smile where a baby tooth once sat, Aislyn saw the two cherry red discs, and a third candy poking from between the fingers of his left hand.

"Rónán!" she repeated over the boy's laughter. "How many times have I told you, no sweets before bed?"

Before Rónán could react, Aislyn snatched the third cherry disc from her son's grasp and popped it into her own mouth. This sent Rónán into a fit of giggles, Aislyn could not help giggling too. She scooped her son off his feet and into her arms, though, at nine years old, he was practically too tall and too heavy for that now.

As she carried him up the stairs to the room they shared above the shop, she heard the crackle and smelled the sugar of the candy in his cheek. Aislyn put her son to bed and handed him his stuffed seal. Soon after his birth, she had sewn and stuffed the animal with scrap fabrics. It was a mismatched patchwork of pattern and color, but Rónán cherished it. He would not close his eyes without it. As he lay there, hugging his seal to his chest, Rónán looked up at his mother as she gently stroked his hair.

Aislyn savored these moments, the sweet candy in her cheek, the soft red hair between her fingers, the music of her son's giggles playing in her ears. After a few moments, she started to sing him a lullaby, the same one that cradled her to sleep as a girl—a tale about seeing the moon and the moon looking back. She continued stroking the top of his head, and when the sound of his breath became low and long, she knew he had floated off to sleep.

Aislyn waited long enough to watch out for the cracked eyelids and mischievous giggles of a boy faking sleep, but none came. She tiptoed down the stairs, carefully hopping over the third to last step that always groaned loudly to avoid waking her son. In the shop, she ensured that everything was in its place and ready for another day of work ahead tomorrow. She tidied the crumpled piles of Rónán's practice projects and returned bolts of fabric to the walls where they usually hung. At the back of the shop, just before the painted door that led to the alleyway, was a small changing room, just big enough for one person. Rónán liked to turn it into his own personal hideaway, so she opened the door to ensure nothing was secreted behind it.

When she was satisfied with the cleanliness and order of her shop, Aislyn grabbed a palmful of blue, yellow, and white flowers sitting in a jar near the front window and made her way to the door. Feeling the warm air rush in as the door cracked open, Aislyn gently cradled the bell above the door to keep it from ringing and waking her son. With an exhale, she returned to her rocking chair, *lowering herself on the seat to watch the black water of the bay for a few quiet moments, but in the darkness, an image played in her mind.*

Nine years ago, just as the sun was setting over the bay, she had heard a knock on her door. Mr. Francis stood there red-eyed and puffy-faced, wringing his old cloth hat between his fingers, as the preacher and the preacher's wife stood like statues on either side of him. She held her stomach—Rónán was still just a movement in her belly—and kept her face still as she learned that her husband had sank with his ship sometime in the darkness of early morning.

She had wanted to cry, to kick, to scream, but she couldn't. Instead, she thanked them for letting her know, and she closed the shop door without waiting for their replies. Aislyn started to do the only thing that seemed to make sense to her amidst the flooding chaos inside of her: she sewed. For days on end, she made clothes and blankets and anything else she could think of, lined with the Ogham blessings she learned from her mother. Then, a month later, she looked down at the redheaded babe that looked up at her with the same emerald eyes as her husband's.

There was so much joy. There was so much grief, and there was another kind of ache. The remembrance that she, too, was fated to leave her son—make him an orphan. Every day, she prayed that the day of her death was far away, but her magic only went so far.

Aislyn started braiding the stems of the flowers, using a needle and thread to secure them together with her signature stitching. Every year on the anniversary of her husband's death, she dropped a wreath of flowers into the bay whispering prayers and humming blessings, with nothing to accompany her but her memory and the moonlight. Now she worked in the darkness, crafting this offering to her husband's resting place.

A sudden, strange noise caught her attention. Nights like this were usually filled with sounds that the people of Bridewater took for granted—the cacophonic chorus of bullfrogs, the droning hum of insects, the lapping splashes of the bay—but this noise was foreign.

A slight, almost imperceptible whimper, somehow both soft and sharp, like a dog crying out after getting its tail trampled, cut through the evening air. Something about the noise caused the hair on the back of Aislyn's neck to prickle, the cool breeze made cold by this pained moan. As she listened again for the sound between the usual refrains of swamp life, a thought percolated at the back of her mind.

The bride of Bridewater.

Aislyn had of course heard the stories of the legend, the namesake of the bay, the tragedy of the drowned bride, the young woman who roamed the streets of town crying, hunting for the fiancé who wronged her. It was a tale husbands laughed about over beer and a fable wives told their children to scare them into line, but Aislyn never put much thought into the stories. Because after all, that is all the tale was—a story.

Isn't it? she thought.

The crying sound continued. Aislyn searched her memories, trying to place the unfamiliar sound. It was not unheard of for a dying deer who barely escaped the maw of a gator to wander into town from the surrounding swamps, moaning its last mournful cry before succumbing to its injuries. But she saw no usual signs in the deep grooves of the street—no hoof prints, no blood.

She heard it again, though this time it sounded different, muffled. Even dampened, but more urgent, hushing the wildlife with its gravity. Even the waters of the bay seemed to still.

Goosebumps trickled up Aislyn's arms. She felt her palms go moist. The sound continued, an unusual, pained groaning growing more desperate the longer it went on. Aislyn held her breath, straining so hard to listen for the cries that she could hear the low hum of her own blood.

Her chest shook, quaking with every beat of her heart. Aislyn darted her eyes back and forth across the empty, black road, looking for any sign of movement. Then, Aislyn looked ahead through the darkness, and a slight flicker of movement caught her eye.

Toward the end of the large wooden dock across from her storefront, she saw an unnatural wavering mass silhouetted by the moon over the bay. The single gas lamp that stood at the mouth of the dock cast an eerie shadow over whatever was convulsing at the end. It reminded Aislyn of an animal trying to claw its way out of a sack with movements both arrhythmic and sporadic.

Taking a deep, shaking breath, Aislyn gripped the floral wreath in her hand and started slowly moving toward the disturbance. With each step, the sounds of the groaning grew louder.

Ice water ran through her veins. She did not remove her eyes from the groaning, thrashing mass.

As she got closer, she strained, squinting her eyes to try to comprehend what she was seeing in the darkness. The languished lowing of whatever she was seeing made her chest hurt. Then, in a flicker of moonlight she finally saw what was calling out to her in the darkness. The whimpers were smothered by Aislyn's own screams, which filled her ears and drowned out all other noises of the night.

Chapter 1: 1887

A soft roll of thunder reverberated over the waters of Bridewater Bay, signaling the start of a new day. Rónán awoke, stretching away the night's sleep. Still lying in the bed, he massaged his neck as he watched the linen drapes hanging over his window spring to life with the intermittent flashes of lightning. Summer storms were not uncommon in the bay. They formed in the swirling humid air over the waters in a blink and dissipated just as quickly. A small puddle of water sat on the windowsill streaming in from the crack he'd left open for a cool night's breeze. Even through the rain, he could feel the thick, warm air floating into his room, hinting that the day would be just as morbidly hot and heavy as it was the day before.

Rónán pushed himself up from the bed and padded across the room, the planks beneath his feet creaking and groaning with each step. He dropped himself onto the short wooden stool in front of his mother's old vanity. The dressing table had been a wedding gift from his father, lovingly crafted from discarded applewood with an antique mirror framed in bronze affixed to the top. The vanity had sat in this corner of the room for as long as Rónán could remember, but neither his mother nor father had gazed out from the looking glass in years. As Rónán rubbed the sleep from his eyes, he took in his own image in the ovoid mirror perched atop the vanity. His orange hair, pale skin, and splash of freckles met his gaze as his green eyes attempted to blink themselves awake. He knew if his mother were here, she would probably bemoan how skinny he'd become, fussing over him while trying to feed him bowls of porridge and stew.

Rónán reached up to tidy the sleep out of his red hair, long enough now to brush the tops of his shoulders. As he did, he got a brief flash of his mother. It had been nearly ten years since he last spoke to her or felt her embrace. He sometimes found it hard to recall the details of her face, but when looking at himself, a spark of recognition would often ignite in the depths of his brain. Sometimes he thought, or perhaps wished, that it was her staring back at him in that mirror. As he pulled his hair back into a knot low on the back of his head, he felt a slight jitter in his hands.

Closing his eyes and taking a deep breath, Rónán curled his fingers into his palms, trying to calm his nerves. He could not recall when his anxiousness started, but he could also not remember a time when he was free from its shackles. He usually steadied his hands by burying himself in his work, but just pulling threads through fabrics and creating garments reminded him of his mother.

After Aislyn disappeared nearly ten years ago, Rónán continued where she had left off, as if he had a choice to do otherwise. The first morning he woke up alone, he had descended to the shop and found it empty. Everything was in place—bolts of fabrics against the back wall, jars of leafy, overgrown plants in the windows, and brown bottles of herbal tinctures behind the counter. The door at the front of the shop was unlocked, but nothing was missing except for his mother. The only thing that resembled her was the lone dress form mannequin that stood still as a statue behind the counter. It was not unusual for Aislyn to be making deliveries in the early morning. She usually sent herself or Rónán out before the heat of the sun made Bridewater too sweltering to traverse. So, Rónán had waited and, to make the time pass quicker, begun to work.

Rónán was so well trained in his mother's craft, that he could practically see where Aislyn left off in a project, even if they had not discussed it. For hours, then days, then weeks, he cut, and hemmed, and basted. He fought hunger pains with bright-colored candies and foraged root vegetables, waiting for her to return. He knew something was wrong, but without a father, Rónán didn't know who to tell. It was in these moments that the tremors in his hands started, softly, slightly at first, but eventually, they became as pronounced and obvious as the freckles on his face.

Whether fortunately or unfortunately for Rónán, he was unsure, it took the people of Bridewater even longer to realize the ethereal Irish woman, with her long, plaited hair and bonneted head, was no longer around. Rónán and his mother were never close to their neighbors, and Bridewater was small enough that there was no official schoolhouse for the children. For the few children who resided in Bridewater, Sunday lessons of eternal promise and fiery perdition were still common at the Baptist church, but Rónán never once attended.

Sometimes, he would sit at the window and watch other children passing through the road to the chapel, smiling, laughing, and teasing one another. He would look toward them, with knots of self-pity and longing in his heart. Sometimes he thought to himself that he would join their merry parade, but that day never came. Instead, he sat alone, inside his shop, watching and working. When enough jobs ran uncharacteristically late and the boy was seen making every delivery with no sign of his mother, the people of Bridewater grew curious. They would walk in front of the shop windows, throwing casual glances inside, or if they were feeling braver, they'd knock on the door and try to squeeze their sweating heads through the small crack Rónán opened to speak with them. No one wanted to make their concern too obvious. Of course, the old hens would cluck about the poor, orphaned boy, bemoaning the tragedy of such a young child left to fend for himself, but their self-righteous squawking only went so far. They seemed content enough to leave the boy alone, and so they did.

Now nineteen, Rónán had lived the last decade mostly alone, his days consumed with sewing, laundering, and making deliveries, while his nights he spent in his bed, recalling the stories his mother used to tell him as he hugged his stuffed seal to his chest. Whether from pity or guilt, the town managed to give Rónán enough work to be self-sufficient. Between his meager wages, trades he made from his shop, and his mother's lessons in foraging edible swamp plants, he managed to survive.

When the pains of sadness for his mother overcame him, he fought them back by locking most of her personal goods into a wooden birch chest that sat at the foot of his bed. As he grew older, Rónán found that the memories of his mother were less frequent, but the pain of loneliness still crept along his insides, like an infection. There were two other people in Bridewater close to his age—the butcher's brother who worked at the docks, and the Creole girl who helped run the general store—but Rónán really only knew their faces, just speaking with them in passing while running errands or making deliveries. Vague memories spun in his mind of giggling over a game of hopscotch or kicking around a tan leather ball with more children in his youth, but the unforeseen illness that rocked Bridewater a decade ago claimed a number of the young and old alike. Somehow, he and his mother were spared from the ravages of the flu, but Rónán did remember her keeping herself busy delivering bottles of her home-brewed, medicinal liquids.

A cool splash of water to his face brought Rónán's attention back from the flood of childhood memories. He cupped another palmful of water to his face and attempted to scrub the sad memories away that clung to him like dried mud. Checking himself once more in the mirror, he pulled on a basic, white cotton, button-down shirt and a pair of taupe linen trousers—both of which he had made, of course—and headed out of his room, down the stairs to his shop.

Half-finished remnants of the previous night were draped across every surface in the shop. A freshly dyed cornflower blue cotton gown hung on the dress form to be hemmed, the butcher's thick, woolen pants imbued with rust-colored stains of animal blood sat on the countertop awaiting a patch, and several bolts of fabric lay haphazardly strewn in the only cushioned chair he owned. Relaxing his shoulders, Rónán ran through mental lists of what he needed to accomplish before the end of the day.

Rónán stepped toward the windows that lined the whole front wall of his shop. He threw back the curtains, blanketing the room in a dim, cool light cast by the slowly dying storm outside. His shop was modest, but Rónán felt that these windows made it priceless. His views of the bay and the busy hum of the docks helped him pass the day. He often found his gaze and his thoughts wandering to the scenes playing right in front of him. Even if he did not interact with his neighbors much, he enjoyed watching glimpses of their lives as they walked to and fro in Bridewater. He looked toward the waters still darkly churning in the bay. Though there were still soft echoes of thunder, the rain had nearly subsided to a soft, arrhythmic patter against the glass. Rónán knew that this day would soon be filled with the white, oppressive heat of June, so he gathered his deliveries and set out into Bridewater, with the tinny chime of the bell overhead.

Rónán locked the door behind him, shaking it gently to be sure it was fastened tight. Crime in Bridewater was practically nonexistent outside of heat-induced, drunken spats, but something about securing his space from the rest of the world put him more at ease. He took an immediate right, making his way down the wooden boardwalk.

He passed in front of Mr. Francis' office, the man whose family had built and managed the docks decades ago. His building was painted a dark, turquoise color, which at one time served as a reminder that the Francises were the closest thing to a rich family that Bridewater had, but the color had ruddied and cracked years ago, hinting at their dwindling coffers.

The next building he came to read "Duvall Family Butcher" in peeling, ornamental lettering. Douglas Duvall, the butcher, lived in a modest apartment above the shop with his wife Clementine, and his younger brother Abel. Rónán snuck a glance into the window of the butchery, seeing hanging meats and garlands of sausages, but no one looked back. Finally, he passed in front of a small boarding house managed by an old spinster woman whose name escaped him. She usually rented out rooms to sailors, but she, like Rónán, received only enough business to stay afloat. All of these buildings in Bridewater still served their primary purposes, but the peeling paint and warped windows hinted at more prosperous pasts.

Though it was still early, Bridewater Bay began to stir with life. Wagons worked their way toward the docks, churning deep grooves into the mud created by the morning storms, flecks of light danced on the ground where the sun peeked through the thinning clouds, and the men of Bridewater yawned and stretched their way toward the docks to begin their work.

As Rónán rounded the corner of the boardinghouse, he made his way toward the general store. There was really only one road in Bridewater, and it formed a big rectangle around the two rows of aging shops. The backs of the shops faced each other, with a wet, grassy alleyway between them. Lines of homes sat on the other side of the rectangular road, some of which just barely seemed to keep the rot of the swamp out of their wooden walls. There was a small stable tucked onto the end of the row of homes where a handful of painted mares huffed and stamped. Next to the stable, the road trailed its way out of Bridewater through miles of bayou, to a tumbledown post office. Rónán wasn't sure how long it had been since any parcels actually passed through its walls. Besides, can it still be called a post office without a postmaster?

The Baptist church and a small cemetery lay on the opposite side of town from where Rónán currently walked. It had stood there for years. But the fourth side of the rectangular road contained the open bay and the docks. That was probably Rónán's favorite side, and he considered himself lucky that his shop faced the salty waters. He spent many nights watching the sky over the bay fade to black, finding something calming and hypnotic about the rippling waves. Bridewater's aging buildings and dwindling traffic gave Rónán the distinct impression that the town was slowly dying, withering like an old hollow oak tree. If it weren't for the proud people of Bridewater determined to hold onto some semblance of the town's former glory, Bridewater would have sunk into the swamps years ago.

Rónán finally reached the front of the general store and pushed the front door open. He was greeted by a round man with a puffy red face. Mr. Hebert was always pleasant, perhaps too pleasant, and he always seemed to have a fidgety enthusiasm. The way he would move around the shop in animated movements and barely meet Rónán's eyes gave Rónán the impression of a young child with too much banked energy and not enough ways to spend it. He always wore a look on his face as if he were thinking of the perfect joke to greet visitors with. For years, he would laugh and tell anyone who would listen that he would soon line his marquis with electric bulbs—*just you wait and see*—but they never seemed to materialize. Despite Hector's slight awkwardness, Rónán thought of the older man as genuinely kind. Perhaps he, more than others, showed Rónán kindness after his mother's disappearance in his own spirited ways. Though he did not take Rónán in, he often gave him more than was agreed upon in trade for his tailoring services. He also seemed to keep a closer watch on the young man than the rest of the town.

"*Bonjour*, Rónán," the man said, smiling through his bristle mustache. "How are you, *mon fils*?"

"Hello, Mr. Hebert," Rónán replied. "I have your washing here."

Rónán reached into his burlap sack and removed a few white aprons and a beige dress belonging to the man's daughter, embroidered with ornamental stitches on the bodice. He neatly stacked them near the shopkeeper's till.

"Ah, *merci, merci*! Helene will be happy to have it returned," Mr. Hebert said, gesturing toward the gown. "I don't know if you have heard, but she is leaving soon."

Even Rónán, loner that he was, managed to hear enough whispers around town to know that the shopkeeper's daughter was leaving soon for a college for Black girls near Atlanta. No one could think of leaving Bridewater for an extended period of time nor could anyone spend a large amount of money without everyone in town knowing their business, but he indulged the man's excitement by shaking his head no.

"She is off to school! She is going to make me and Henriette so proud," the man beamed, curling his mustache up toward his ears. Even now, he seemed to address the space behind Rónán rather than the boy himself.

"*C'est magnifique*!" Even as he said it, Rónán wanted to shrink inside himself. He didn't speak French. The all-too-familiar knot in his gut tightened.

If the shopkeeper noticed Rónán's embarrassment, he allowed it to pass unacknowledged.

Instead, he cleared his throat and in his own shame addressed Rónán.

"*Mons fils*, could you?" Hector eyed a small tear in the seam of his left sleeve, and Rónán understood. As he pulled a rolled leather case from the pocket of his trousers, retrieving a needle and thread from inside, Mr. Hebert laughed and exclaimed, "You'll never catch a good tailor without his needle, no?"

Rónán smiled and quickly fixed the rip with a simple ladder stitch, knotting the ends of the thread to hold the seams of Hector's shirt in place again. The older man examined his work, giving a small tug on the sleeve as if to check that the new stitches would hold. When they did, Hector handed Rónán his payment and included a small bag of candies for his trouble. Rónán immediately recognized the familiar red discs. Cherry was always his favorite.

"Thank you," Rónán said, tucking the payment and small bag of candies into the sack hanging over his shoulder.

"Let me know if you need anything else," Mr. Hebert said as he gestured to his eclectic assortment of wares. "I need to place another order soon from New Orleans. If you need anything for the shop, you just let me know."

Mr. Hebert acted as a somewhat hands-off mentor to Rónán. He would usually help Rónán to place orders for fabrics, threads, and notions from the larger haberdasheries in New Orleans, but Rónán was still stocked from his last order. He bowed his head in appreciation of Hector's kindness, nonetheless.

"I have more deliveries to get to. Please give Mrs. Hebert and Helene my well wishes," Rónán said.

Without another word, Rónán turned and made his way out of the shop. The sun had slowly burned away more of the storm clouds as he stood talking with Mr. Hebert, making the day both brighter and hotter than when he had entered the general store. Over the next hour, in the rising heat, he continued his deliveries, stopping just long enough to trade his completed works for the agreed upon sums.

Walking back toward the tailor shop in the heat that blanketed Bridewater, Rónán gazed at the long and muddy grooves protruding in the roads. There was something artistic in the chaos of the mud sculptures that lined the street, with their deep brown grooves and cracked edges from baking in the Louisiana sun. It was like a mini mountain range right outside his front door. While looking at the peaks and valleys of the furrowed road, he could not shake the familiar feeling of being watched. Whether it was his own anxieties or just the nature of living and working in a small town, Rónán often felt eyes on him. The buildings, the trees, the people—they all seemed to watch his every movement. He tried to shake the feeling, and he did not dare glance over his shoulder for fear of making eye contact with one of his neighbors. Instead, he straightened his back and continued walking.

To his right, the docks buzzed like a colony of bees as the work picked up. A ship, too large to approach the coast, anchored in the bay a few hundred feet out beyond the docks. A small, wooden rowboat, manned by a single worker, made its way back and forth from the ship to the docks, gliding across the water like a duck, carrying boxes and crates of goods to the workers waiting to unload. Crates were moved from boat to dock and then from dock to wagon before they began their journey on the veins of roads connecting this part of the state.

Rónán entered his shop, brushing the dirt from his shoes on the mat right inside the doorway. He removed the gunny sack from his side, tossing the now empty bag onto the floor near the windows. A pang of hunger gnawed at his insides, so he popped a cherry sweet into his mouth, and ripped a small piece off a loaf of bread that a customer gave him during his delivery run. He thought of supplementing his meal with a piece of cheese, the salty kind made by the butcher's wife Clementine, but he wanted to get to work. The steady feeling of being watched brought the tremor back to his hands. The best way to quiet that part of him was to bury himself in his sewing.

Rónán got to work. His stitching never seemed quite as neat as his mother's, but he also was forced to continue honing his skill alone without her more practiced guidance after she disappeared. As he sewed, warm memories of his mother's humming would play in his ears. He would sometimes hum her lullabies to himself, but in this, too, he lacked her skill. Aislyn's light, lilting voice carried into her music, sweetening every melody that passed her lips. He missed her music, and if he thought about it too long, crashing waves of grief would drown out any song he tried to produce.

Just as much as he missed her singing, Rónán missed her tales. In animated voices and crescendoing tones, she would spin stories of selkies, seals, mermaids, and butterflies that she had learned as a girl in Ireland. Rónán could sit at her heels for hours with vivid images dancing in his head as she sang and told fairytales of fantastical creatures.

When his mind wandered away from the stories and music, Rónán often found his eyes trailing toward the docks. As he sewed and hemmed, he watched the workers loading, unloading, and organizing cargo. He also found himself drawn to the same worker, a blonde and muscular boy. He recognized this boy, well now this young man, as the butcher's younger brother Abel.

Rónán and Abel were not unfamiliar with one another. They often saw each other in passing, while making deliveries, or going about life in Bridewater. They were in fact the only two boys their own age in the town. Though they were cordial, Rónán would not say they were friends, not that he would necessarily call himself friends with anyone in Bridewater.

Abel was the type of person who always seemed to be in a pleasant mood. His boyish, round eyes glowed as they gave unwavering attention to whomever he was speaking with. Even if Rónán ran into him after a long day of work at the docks, Abel seemed to exist to smile. Today, Rónán could hear his laughter floating over the drumming noise of the docks. Perhaps that is what caught his attention at first, but it was something else that kept it.

Rónán wasn't quite sure why, but he kept finding himself distracted by the young man. The way he endlessly worked without ever seeming tired, how he threw his head back after a joke, and how he carried himself among the other men working the docks though he was the youngest by a decade—it all captivated Rónán.

As he watched Abel work, Rónán, for the third time that day, felt a pang in the pit of his stomach, like someone plucked a harp string and left it resonating in his gut. Though, there was something different about this feeling. It wasn't like the familiar bruise of hunger or anxiety; it was something else, something warmer, something he had not felt since he was with his mother. It was like the sparkle in her eyes the last time she smiled down at him as she worked in her rocking chair with the sea breeze blowing her hair. It had been so long since Rónán felt this, that it almost felt wrong, foreign. The tug in his chest made him stop to catch his breath.

His hands shook again. He stretched and flexed his fingers to try to steady them, but it was not enough. Then, he felt a small, heated pressure at the corner of his eyes, and he realized that for the first time in he didn't know how long, he was crying.

He felt alone. That momentary feeling he got while gazing at Abel bubbled from warmth to anger.

How could ma leave me? he thought. *Why did she leave me?*

He wiped his nose on the cuff of his sleeve with a protracted sniff. An immediate guilt snuffed out his anger, and that guilt cooled into sadness. As he sat there, his insides storming with emotions, he realized it was late in the day. The dock workers had wrapped up their work and, trading handshakes and pats on the back, had parted ways for the evening.

Dabbing the corners of his eyes to blot away the tears, Rónán began to tidy the shop, trying to take note of his morning priorities, but he found it hard to focus. With a deep breath, he closed the curtains, obscuring his view of the bay. Then, he opened the front door of the shop and made his way to the porch.

Under the awning, his mother's old wooden rocking chair sat exactly where she left it before she disappeared. Rónán's father had made it for her, and it was her favorite place to work. Sometimes he thought about moving it, trying to protect it from the elements in the bay, but Rónán had been scared to bring it inside. He feared that if he moved the lonely chair, it meant that his mother would never come back. Instead, he left it there, empty, as an open invitation, as a prayer, that he would one day come down from his room to see her again, rocking and singing to herself as she watched over the waters.

Tonight, he decided to sit there. He wanted to remember her. He needed to remember her.

Of all the places in Bridewater, he felt closest to her in this softly swaying chair.

Closing his eyes and leaning his head back, he began to hum a familiar melody. An old, Irish blessing she had ingrained in him as a child. She often spoke of the importance of remembering where they came from and holding on to certain parts of his past, so he did what he could. He longed to see his mother again, to hear her voice, to share his stories. She needed to know how her boy managed to survive all these years.

He did not know how long he had sat there humming to himself, eyes closed, but it felt like both an eternity and an instant. Sitting in the darkness, Rónán felt the familiar feeling of being watched creeping back up his spine like a bug. He imagined pairs of eyes fixed on him from the dark space between his shop and Mr. Francis' offices. Another voice in his head tried to convince him that someone was standing just beyond the trees near the chapel. Despite the heat of the day and the lingering, heavy humidity, Rónán grew cold. With a shiver, he opened his eyes.

As his vision adjusted to the darkness, Rónán looked up and down the muddy road along the bay. No one was stirring, and no unusual noises leapt from the stillness of the night. But Rónán could not shake the feeling that somewhere nearby in the creeping darkness, someone or something was watching him. He held his breath, waiting for someone to appear, some shape to take form from out of the darkness to his left or right, his head now reeling with images from childhood nightmares. He strained his ears to hear something, anything really, but nothing seemed to stir.

Then he saw it; out past the docks, there was something still, unmoving in the water, unusually still. Against the oily black water of the bay, the silhouette could only be seen in brief blinks of reflected moonlight.

Rónán concentrated his eyes on the stillness, trying to make sense of the dark shape he was seeing. It was round, barely cresting from the top of the water. Something about the way the object remained motionless in the churning water of the bay bit at Rónán, causing the hairs to stand up on the back of his neck as if he just plunged into deep, icy waters after a day in the sun.

The shape didn't even bob in the water like a normal floating thing would. Something about its stillness made him picture gators playing. It wasn't unheard of for one of those swamp-dwellers to make it to the bay, but it was rare, the salty water being too much for them to tolerate. Rónán stood and walked closer to the water's edge, placing each foot carefully, firmly, as if trying to dodge hidden holes. He squinted his eyes, trying to narrow his focus.

With each of Rónán's soft, careful steps, the shape started to grow unnaturally. Rónán wanted to look away, but he couldn't. He slowed his steps, his head roiling trying to make sense of the shape. To his horror, Rónán realized, whatever he was looking at wasn't growing. It was rising out of the depths of the bay.

An aggressive beating sounded in Rónán's head as his heart struggled to escape from his sinewy muscles and bones. Blood roared in his ears and his gaze was locked on the thing—the creature—rising out of the water. It moved slowly, revealing itself inch-by-inch. Steadily the thing continued to rise from the black void that was the sea.

A cloud started to form in the water around the shape, disrupting the moonlit reflections. The fog around the shape grew, like dropping a muddy rock into the water creating ripples of sludge as the dirt washed from the rock's surface. But this was different. It was not mud; it was not even a cloud.

It was *hair*.

The waterlogged hair wound its way around what he now knew, with a gasp, to be a head. Ice shot through his veins, paralyzing

Rónán where he stood at the edge of the water, but gray, bloated skin continued to emerge inch after inch, like some old sunken ship pulled piece by piece from the sea floor. The hair fell in front of the face like a veil.

Rónán wanted to scream. He wanted to run, but all he could do was look on in horror as this thing surfaced. In a brief flash of moonlight, Rónán could see the creature's eyes, or rather, where its eyes should be. There was something wrong, something unnatural about where the eyes sat. The sockets were dark and bruised, and the eyelids were sewn shut with jagged, crude, angry stitches.

As if he got punched in the gut, Rónán was finally freed from the trance of fear that held him frozen. He thrust his hands up to his eyes as if to free stitches from his own eyes, but instead, he was trying to rub the vision of this thing, this woman, away. Suddenly dizzy, he doubled over on the shore, a sickly heat churning in his stomach. He held his breath, trying to keep the contents of his stomach inside his body, when now suddenly at eye level with the creature rising from the water, he heard a faint noise rise over the lapping sounds of the bay.

A soft but shrill uneven hissing filled the air. It was quiet but overlaid with a wet, gurgling noise, as if a snake were spitting and writhing in a boiling pot. There was something sinister about the noise. As if putting the whole rest of the world to sleep, the woman's whispering started to drown out every other midnight sound in Bridewater. Rónán tried to plug his ears, but the whispering still leaked through. He tried singing his mother's blessing again, but even that could not compete with the hissing. It continued to grow louder in his ear, as if it were coming from inside his own head.

Everything about the noise felt wrong. Rónán was about to scream—to beg it to stop, to scream to his neighbors for help— when it quieted as quickly as it started.

Rónán unplugged his ears and lifted his head. With ragged breaths, Rónán forced air into his lungs, and he began shaking violently, as if he were caught naked in a snowstorm. Slowly, nervously, he opened his eyes.

There was nothing. The woman was gone, her song no more.

With a jerk as if he were prodded with a hot iron, Rónán stood and sprinted back across the street toward the tailor shop, narrowly avoiding tripping on the deep grooves worn into the earth by wagon wheels. The door slammed heavily behind Rónán, and he latched it with a definitive click of the lock. Heaving as if he had run for hours, Rónán put his back toward the door and doubled over. He blinked a few times, trying to convince himself he was safe inside. A hot, salty tear rolled down his cheek, and his hands began to tremble. Then, without looking back, he hurried away from the door and up the stairs to his room.

Chapter 2

Rónán stared at the ceiling as the silver shimmer of moonlight faded into the honeydew mist of another morning. His wooden bed frame creaked and cracked in protest as he turned his body throughout the night in bed. Fighting to get comfortable, Rónán struggled to sleep. Part of him didn't even want to. Every time he closed his eyes, tendrils of hair stretched out through the darkness, droning whispers sounded in his ears, and bloodied, stitched eyes darted back and forth from behind their closed lids. Rónán was afraid of what else might come to him in the dark if he shut his eyes for too long.

As if his body were filled with the briny muck of the swamps, he slowly pushed himself up from his bed. Glancing in the vanity, Rónán saw the discolored skin around his eyes, bags of mottled pink and purple. He splashed cool water against his face in a vain attempt to bring energy to his tired body. The red waves of his hair framed his face. He knew he looked wild and unkempt, but pulling his hair back would take more effort than he could give in the moment. His muscles ached from lack of sleep and the bitter acid of fear that had paralyzed them yesterday.

In a burst of light, Rónán struck a match to ignite the weathered cook stove that sat against the wall opposite his bed. With a clatter, he sat a tarnished, silver pot down on the cookstove to bring it to a boil. Rónán usually used coffee beans as a makeshift dye for small swatches of clothing or thread. This wasn't his preferred method; it was a last resort for when he had trouble foraging other, better plants to make the rich, earthy yellow dyes. His mother described how to use the various plants and even the coffee in one of the many leatherbound notebooks she left behind. The books were lined with neatly written notes and quickly scratched illustrations explaining how and where to find certain plants to use in the shop—some medicinal, some practical, and others edible. However, today, he wasn't thinking of his mother's quick-fix suggestion for yellow dye. Instead, he needed the extra jolt of alertness that the brown brew would bring.

The sound of soft bubbles filled the room, signaling that the water had begun to boil. Rónán quickly extinguished the flames of the cook stove—the June morning was already proving to be hot—and tossed a handful of ground beans into the pot. As he waited and his room filled with the earthy, smoky smell of the coffee, Rónán bit into a crusty end of the remaining bread he had saved from the previous day. The buttery, soft inside and the cornmeal crunch on the outside only made him more aware of the hunger pains gurgling in his stomach. So, this time, he unwrapped the goat cheese given to him by the butcher's wife, unknotting the twine and peeling back the sheer white fabric protecting the cheese. He tore at the corner of the block, not bothering to neatly cut a piece, and added it to the bites of bread already in his mouth. He savored the salty, tangy flavor.

When the liquid on the stove became a deep, murky brown, he mugged a cup full out of the silver pot. Carefully bringing the cup to his lips, he sipped, instantly feeling the warmth radiate through his chest as it traveled down to his gut. He didn't love the grittiness of coffee prepared haphazardly this way or how it habitually made the jitters in his hands worse, but there was something comforting about the drink. He would have to remember to ask Mr. Hebert if he had any cinnamon sticks the next time he visited the general store.

Rónán sat for a few moments, enjoying his sparse meal. He knew it would likely be his only meal of the day, but without his mother around to playfully bemoan how skinny he was,

Rónán didn't think much of it. He was used to making do with less. He would save some of the cheese for later, and maybe he would stop by the butcher shop later to see what, if any, meat he could afford to buy. If he were able to secure something from Douglas, he might even make a stew, an old recipe of his mother's containing a boiled concoction of swamp potatoes, carrots, and whatever meat they could get. If he were lucky, maybe Douglas would have some spare fatty lamb.

He continued to wonder if he imagined what he saw the previous night at the water's edge. As he did, the same tendrils of ice that crept up his spine the night before started to lick at his lower back. He shook his head, sending his red hair flying around his face. He couldn't think about that today. He needed to work. Still trying to shake the thought free from the snare in his mind, Rónán walked down the stairs to his shop, but in some dimly lit corner of his brain, he could still hear that light hissing, gurgling noise that came from the woman's sewn mouth.

His shoulders rising and falling in deep breaths, Rónán entered his workspace, seeing the remnants from the previous day strewn around the shop. He pulled back the drapes, washing the room in a warm cascade of orange light. Resting just outside of his front door, in view of the window, sat a lumpy brown bag. He knew it to be filled with various linens from the Baptist church. About once a week, the preacher's wife, a plump older woman, would drop off what needed laundering. Though Rónán didn't speak with the preacher or his wife, he could tell from splotchy, violet stains snaking through the cotton that the preacher was all too fond of the communion wine.

There was an unspoken agreement between Rónán and the preacher's wife, both figuratively and literally. Rónán knew part of his payment was the fact that the preacher and his wife generally left him alone, not proselytizing him or asking him for tithes. Moreover, the preacher's wife always included a sock filled with a few, sparse copper coins that had no doubt previously sat in the offering basket some Sunday afternoon. She almost always left her deliveries on the porch before he woke up. Rónán couldn't recall a time that he had exchanged words with her, not that he minded much. He would boil, scrub, and wring her husband's vestments nonetheless, and return them as wordlessly as they were left in front of the tailor shop.

Rónán leaned half outside the front door as he heaved the large bag inside, thinking to himself that he didn't have the supplies he needed to get the contents clean. Even halfway out the door, Rónán felt the hazy, wet heat start to make him sweat. The bright sun already threatened to make this June day unbearable. He decided it was best to begin his day once again by making deliveries. He gathered the newly patched trousers of the butcher, grabbed a small glass bottle, and began to walk toward the shop that stood two doors down.

Deep troughs ran along the entire length of the road, as if someone had spent the night plowing lines into the dirt in front of the shops. Wagon wheels had worked the grooves so thoroughly into the ground that Rónán could tell the road would stay this way until the next rain. Knowing the unpredictability of the weather in Bridewater, the next rain could be any moment. If they remained dried this way for too long, the roads in front of the docks would become nearly impassable. When they did, Rónán would hear a chorus of heaves and grunts as the workers tried to muscle free whatever was caught in a groove.

During Rónán's short walk to the Duvall butchery, Bridewater was waking up, humming with life. He watched as familiar strangers passed by and listened to the morning small talk that accompanied them. Whinnying from the stables on the other side of town cut into the forenoon song. There was no urgency in the movement of the townspeople, which felt strange to Rónán after his own eventful evening. He was still struggling to process everything he had seen and heard, but to those moving to and fro around him, it was just another day in Bridewater.

As the boardwalk creaked underfoot, Rónán's skin buzzed. The familiar, creeping feeling from last night crawled up his neck, as if a bee hovered just above his skin, and Rónán shivered, trying to shake it. Nothing could erase the strange sense of eyes stalking him. There were plenty of men walking to the docks, but Rónán knew it wasn't them he was feeling. Rónán slowed his pace, not wanting to stop completely for fear of what might actually be behind him. As he approached the door of the butcher shop and reached a shaking hand out to turn the doorknob, he heard it again.

As faint but as clear as a mosquito buzzing in his ear, the gurgling, hissing whisper that haunted him the previous evening rose from the salty waters behind him.

Practically entranced by the whispering, Rónán felt as if he no longer had power over his muscles. He was trapped in place, his feet refusing to budge. Rónán's grip tightened on the bottle in his hand, hoping—no yearning—that the solid object would somehow ground him, bring him back into control. He slowly brought his eyes to the glass storefront of the butcher shop, hoping to catch a reflection of whatever was behind him, fearing he would see the woman again. The door of the butcher shop flew open. His attention suddenly snapped back from the storefront window, Rónán stood face-to-face with the butcher's younger brother. Startled, Rónán dropped the brown bottle he clutched in his hand, sending it toppling to the path, bouncing with a percussive beat of wood and glass.

"My apologies," Abel said in his slow, southern drawl.

Stooping low, Abel leaned down to grab the fallen bottle. Sunlight reflected off the boy's sand colored hair, catching Rónán's attention.

As Abel righted himself, he laughed, "My brother says I walk around like I'm flat corned all the time."

Abel looked at Rónán with his round, boyish eyes. Something about the way the sun hit Abel's face made his brown irises shine a bright, honey color. Rónán felt a familiar warmth in his gut, like he just took another long swig of his morning coffee. He stared at Abel, his heart beating so loud he was afraid the other boy would hear it. A prolonged silence sat in the emptiness between them. After what seemed like an eternity, Abel handed the glass bottle back to Rónán with a polite grin. Their fingers brushed slightly, sending an electric spark up Rónán's arm. Rónán felt the red rushing to his cheeks, and he began to speak too quickly, tripping over his own thoughts.

"No," he broke the silence. "I'm sorry—it was my fault. I thought… I thought I heard something behind me. And, I–I wasn't paying attention to where I was walking."

Abel chuckled again, "Well, for what it's worth, I'm sorry anyway. Now, you have a good one."

Abel stood aside, holding the door open with one long arm, allowing Rónán to pass him into the butcher shop. As the door closed behind him and he stepped further into the sun, Abel turned to give another wave and a toothy grin. Again, Rónán felt the blood warm his cheeks, and he was suddenly thankful that the butcher shop was still dimly lit with the curtains drawn shut.

A waft of a coppery iron smell flooded Rónán's nostrils as he walked toward the counter. Douglas Duvall kept his eyes fixed on Rónán, only darting once to take in the form of his brother through the window on the door.

Douglas' eyes always seemed to look right through you. They were a stark bright blue, but rarely did they hold expression, as if he were constantly lost in his own head. Like Abel, Douglas was a tall, broad man, naturally bulky from his work. Unlike Abel, thick, dark hair coated almost every part of Douglas that was visible from his solid arms to his shaggy beard. Douglas, as much as his butcher shop, was a staple in Bridewater Bay. The Duvall family were some of the first to move to the bay when the docks were first built and opened to trade. Some time ago, when Rónán was still a child living with his mother, Douglas married Clementine, the preacher's daughter. Though they did not have kids of their own, they cared for Abel. Douglas was a little more than ten years older than Abel, and the boys lost their parents years ago in the flu that killed its way through Bridewater Bay.

Douglas didn't speak much to Rónán, despite them having traded goods and services since Rónán took over his mother's shop. Rónán had the distinct impression that Douglas didn't talk much to anyone, but if the rest of Bridewater kept Rónán at an arm's length, the butcher kept him at two. Even Clementine, who always reminded Rónán of a rabbit in the ways she twitched and sat quietly in the corner of the shop, barely spoke with Rónán during his deliveries though she would sometimes give him some of her homemade cheeses, keeping her gaze to the floor the entire time.

"Gall?" Douglas asked in his hoarse, husky voice as Rónán passed him the glass bottle.

There were other ways to get grease stains from clothing, but Rónán still swore by the bile that the butcher extracted from a cow's gallbladder. It was, after all, how his mother taught him.

"Yes, sir. Thank you," Rónán said politely. Now he nodded a greeting toward Clementine,

"Ma'am."

The young woman stood quickly, almost jumping from her stool as if it had given her a static shock and accepted the pair of trousers that Rónán held out to her. Without a word, she nodded her own thanks, retreating to the back of the shop seemingly to put away the clothing.

Douglas' cold, blue eyes followed his wife's movements. Then, he looked back at Rónán.

"You'll get it tomorrow," he gruffed.

Then, with a slight tip of his chin which Rónán took as a sign to leave, Douglas angled his head toward the shop door.

Rónán gave a polite, half-smile, returning Douglas's nod, and headed toward the door. As the door shut behind him, he let out a small sigh. Something about interacting with Douglas always made him feel guarded, almost nervous. A slight tremor shook his hands, so Rónán squeezed them into fists at his side as he began making his way home to his shop. As he did so, he looked out over the bay. As much as he tried to quiet his mind, looking at the bay stamped an image of the woman in the water into his brain. Despite his curled fists, the shaking in his hands became more pronounced.

When he was nearly back to his shop, he heard a harsh, dry, scolding sound. Looking up, he saw a blackbird sitting on the awning above his front door. The bird seemed to quiet the closer Rónán got to his home. In a jilted, twitching movement, the bird tilted its head so one eye was squarely facing Rónán. Rónán paused for a moment, looking back at the bird, and felt something unnerving about the black, shining pool that was the bird's eye. Like a string connected their vision, the two sat with their gazes locked on one another. Rónán got the distinct feeling that if the bird could speak, it would say something to him. But what would it say? Had it seen the woman, too? There was just something so unnatural about the still, attentive posture of the bird. A sudden, sharp noise from the docks snapped the string. With another loud call, the bird took flight, leaving the awning behind.

Rónán reentered his shop. Not wanting to be distracted today, or perhaps because he was afraid to look at the bay, he put his back to the window and got to work. What he really loved about tailoring was his ability to create something new. If he could, he would spend his day creating garments for the people of Bridewater, but there simply weren't enough people or enough business in the town for that to be his sole line of work. If he were lucky, someone might want a new smoking jacket or sleeping gown, but more often than not, he supplemented his passion with other services. He spent most days patching knees, stitching hems, and laundering linens. He took in the work that awaited him today, deciding to work on a blouse that needed its worn collar to be replaced. He would wait for the bottle of gall from Douglas before he began the washing,

Rónán spent the rest of his day cutting, hemming, and stitching his way through various projects. He preferred to work by hand. Sewing with a needle and thread may have been slower, but it was one of the only things that could consistently keep his hands busy enough to stifle the tremors. At some point before he was born, his mother obtained a Singer machine, powered by foot. The black iron, ornamented machine sat behind the counter in his workspace, but it was more decor, more exhibit, than anything. He couldn't even recall a time his mother used it.

Despite this, Rónán couldn't fathom the thought of getting rid of the machine. Like many other parts of his shop, it reminded him too much of his mother.

As the sun sank over the horizon, and the water of the bay grew darker, Rónán lit the lamp in his workspace. He was so focused on his project that he didn't even notice the silence, which grew over the street as the workers at the dock filed home for the night. The flickering of his oil lamp put him in a kind of trance; he continued working well into the night, keeping his back turned to the window and the waters beyond.

A crawling, numbing ache spread across his shoulders. Like a flower wilting in the sun, Rónán worked for hours, bending over his sewing, his posture slowly sinking until his spine arched with a soft curve. Rónán stretched out the tension, bringing one ear down to his shoulder and then the other. The light dimmed so much now that his eyes ached from straining to focus. As he rolled his head around at the base of his neck, he looked toward the lamp. Something about the soft glow sparked a memory.

The scene with Abel from in front of the butcher shop replayed in his head, with it a bubble of embarrassment popped in his gut. To be scared in broad daylight was one thing, to be scared in front of a grown man was another. Rónán watched the glass tumble from his hand over and over in his head. He willed himself to catch it, but he couldn't. Even if he wanted to change the past, he knew it wasn't possible. He remembered Abel's friendly grin and the light in his eyes. Rónán had seen Abel many times, but he had never been so close to him. Another feeling twisted with the confusing shame he felt, but he couldn't quite place it. It was like he was walking through the bayou in a thick fog and not being able to see the tree right in front of him. He sensed it, something there beyond his vision, but the image was hazy at the edges.

A burst of lightning and a clap of thunder snapped his attention back to the shop. A light pattering drummed against the roof and walls. Rónán turned toward his windows to watch the storm roll into Bridewater from over the bay. There was something calming about the soft tapping of rain and the echoing thunder over the water. But between the drumming rain and the rolling thunder, there was something else. Rónán's hands shook, and his throat tightened.

He was hearing *it* again.

Somehow, over the storm and through the shop walls, the faint gurgling whisper filled his shop. It was like letting air out of a balloon, and it seemed to trickle in directly under the door and through the cracks in the windowpane.

He shivered. He felt as if someone had dumped a bucket of icy water over his head. Again he tried to calm his hands by clasping them together and gasped as he accidentally pricked his palm with the needle still held in his hand. Even feeling the piercing sting in his palm where blood emerged from his broken skin, Rónán didn't react. He felt paralyzed again.

It's all in your head, Rónán thought.

In his stasis, he could not remove his eyes from the windows. The lamp beside him cast long, eerie reflections that danced on the glass in front of him. Something moved in the shallows. He sensed it before he could see it.

Rónán stared into the blackness, his breath quickening. He tried to focus his eyes. He wanted to make sense of what he was seeing. As slowly as he could, like trying not to scare a rabbit, he leaned closer to the glass. Another flash of lightning illuminated the shallows of the bay. Rónán felt a sickly heat. With another bright crack snaking across the sky, he recognized her ~~dark,~~ shaded, sewn-shut eyes, staring at him through her veil of dripping wet hair.

Thick, warm saliva began flooding Rónán's mouth. He felt as if he were going to be sick, but he still couldn't look away—he couldn't move. Bile churned in his chest.

More lightning. She seemed to be growing again, like yesterday. In the next blast of light, he could see her crooked, broken nose. A roaring pressure sounded in Rónán's ears, and through it, his own heart pounded a hammering beat.

A burst of white lightning illuminated the woman again. In an instant, he got the impression that she was becoming larger, no longer able to be contained in the shallows.

No, he thought. *She is coming closer.*

He watched her move toward him in brief flashes of lightning as if he were watching a scene in a zoetrope. She moved awkwardly and convulsively. There was something inhuman about the way she took each step, as if she were a puppet being controlled by the unsteady hands of a child. He noticed more details with each new blaze of light. Her graying, bloated skin looked rotted, as if a single touch would cause it to slough from her skull. Her face was peppered with bruises. Her black, sopping hair hung in front of her face, as if she were looking at him through a line of trees. Mud dripped from her hairline onto her face giving the impression of blood cascading from her scalp, and her dirty gown hung tattered to her knobby ankles. Her swollen hands were clasped together over her stomach as if she were praying.

No, he thought. *As if she were holding a bouquet.*

She was the bride of Bridewater—the story told to get children to behave and to scare your friends around a campfire. But here she was in the flesh, squelching in the mud, crossing the street to get to Rónán. He had tears in his eyes, but he could not look away. His heart threatened to burst from his chest. He felt hot despite the cold sweat dripping down his back.

Rónán wanted to move. He tried to, but he couldn't, as if it were him trying to struggle through the mud and not the bride. As she grew closer, her whispers became louder. Now, they almost had a frantic edge to them that Rónán hadn't heard before.

The bride crossed the dirt road in front of his shop. Then, with a sickening, wet slapping sound, she lifted one foot onto the wooden plank porch followed by the other. She moved slowly forward, step-by-step, until her face was nearly pressed against the glass of the tailor shop.

Only now, Rónán realized why her voice came out in struggling, gurgling whispers.

There in the flicker of his lamplight, Rónán could see that just as the bride's eyelids were forced shut with wild, uneven stitches, so was her mouth. Only, there was something wrong with the way her mouth was shaped. There was a slackness to her jaw. Rónán had the sick feeling that if he were to undo the stitches on her mouth, her jaw would come tumbling down, tearing away from the rest of her face in a sinewy mass of rotting skin. Only the slightest part in the corner of her mouth where the stitches failed to meet allowed her words to escape. Rónán could see the edge of her blackened blue lips moving, fighting against their restraints. And even though her eyes were fastened shut, Rónán felt them boring directly through his own.

Rónán sobbed now, heaved as if he were fighting to catch a breath before he drowned. Then, with a loud *BOOM* of thunder, Rónán was freed, falling from where he sat as if he were pulled backwards by ghostly hands reaching out from the darkness behind him. Trying to catch himself, Rónán shot his bloody hand out to the side, nicking the oil lamp, sending it crashing to the floor. The room was plunged into total darkness.

His hands were shaking violently now. The pain at the back of his head where it had connected with the floor forced his eyes shut. He strained his ears, listening for the bride's whispers, listening for the sound of her wet feet plodding toward him, but all he could hear now was the rain pattering against his shop and distant rolling thunder.

He grasped for matches in the dark to relight his lamp. He was trembling so violently now, he wasn't sure he could hold his hands steady enough to strike the match. Then, another large flash of lightning illuminated the night. There was nothing. The bride no longer stood with her face pressed to his window.

Taking a deep breath to steady himself, Rónán struck the match with a scrape and a sulfuric flash. His lamp fought against the darkness. With all the bravery he could muster, he moved closer to the window and peered outside. In the dim light of his lamp and the intermittent blaze of lightning outside, he saw something that made his heart momentarily stop beating. On the wooden path in front of his window, caked in the still wet mud, were two footprints, directly where the bride had stood moments before.

Struggling through the tremble causing his fingers and hands to violently jerk, Rónán locked the front door. Not wanting to stand unprotected in the window, he shoved the curtains closed as quickly as he could. He tasted the wet, salty tears that stained his cheeks. He wiped his face with the back of his hands, picked up his oil lamp, and cautiously made his way upstairs.

Chapter 3

Rónán spent a second night in darkness, tumbling in and out of sleep. Visions of the gnarled bride swam in his vision from the moment his head touched the pillow until the roosters outside of the butcher's began screaming their welcome to the new morning. His muscles ached with sleeplessness, so he rubbed the crook in his neck with the palm of his hand. He pushed himself up, still sitting on the edge of the bed. He looked toward the floorboards, where a slender stream of light beamed across the room from under the embroidered drapes over his window. When he was still a boy, Aislyn had worked with him to stitch trees along the curtains in threads of green and gold. The sun illuminated them from behind, giving the impression of a glowing forest fire. He parted the curtains and cracked the window to let out the stale air of his room. Hot, humid air flowed into the stillness of the room. Even for a Louisiana summer morning, the day was already warm.

Rónán pulled his hair back, providing a bit of cool relief to his neck, and stood from his bed, his knees popping with the effort. The sound of his bare feet against the wood syncopated with the whispering sounds of the waters outside his window. Rónán washed his face in the basin nestled into the applewood vanity. For a moment, he didn't recognize who looked back at him in the oblong mirror. The circles under his eyes from nights without sleep had deepened and darkened, expanding like a bruise. The glassy whites of his eyes were spidered in red veins. The aching feeling radiating throughout his neck and shoulders threatened to spread, and if he didn't start sleeping soon, Rónán knew the dull pain would cause him to be all but useless in his own shop. The ladies of Bridewater kept him busy enough, but he couldn't afford to start slacking and losing pay. If there is one lesson he'd learned since his mother left, it was that less work usually translated to more hunger.

Stretching his arms out over his head, Rónán took a deep breath in, then released it slowly with an audible sigh. Hunger pains gnawed at his insides, compounding the body ache. Besides the cheese from Clementine and the bag of candies from Mr. Hebert, his pantry was dwindling. As he bit into the last of the salty, creamy cheese, he made a mental note to forage for swamp potato and carrots next time he made a trip into the bayou. He kept plenty of his own edible plants, planted in a box in the alleyway and in various pots and wooden boxes throughout the shop. Most of them served other purposes. He could use red cabbage in soup or to brighten white clothes, rosemary to flavor his stews or to treat stomach pains, even chamomile to brew some tea or clean a wound. His mother's notebooks detailed it all. She had also been the one to propagate the garden. Like her shop, Rónán only cared for the garden in her absence, hoping one day she'd walk in the door and take over like she had never left. At the thought of his mother, a hollow pit opened in his stomach. He pressed his palms together in front of his chest to still the shake threatening to take hold.

Rónán descended from his room into the shop where he was greeted by the large, burlap bag full of the preacher's clothes that still sat unattended in the front corner. He walked around the counter and opened the store cupboard. His hands groped the dark corners for a box on the upper shelf. When they came back empty, he realized he would need to make another trip to the general store. Not only was he still waiting for his bottle of ox gall from Douglas, but also, his bar of lye soap was about as thin as a matchstick.

Grabbing the bag of copper coins the preacher's wife had left with her laundry, Rónán walked out of his shop door, not bothering to pull back the curtains. As he stepped outside, Rónán stopped in his tracks at the sight of the muddy footprints at the front of his store. He had hoped that he had dreamt the encounter with the bride, that he would wake up and realize it was all a nightmare. But the brown, caked footprints proved that was not the case. He kicked at the prints with the toes of his leather boots, trying to erase them from the porch, but they were still wet from the rain and became two smeared mud pies at the base of the window, marking exactly where the bride had stood the night before.

Looking down at the dark splotches, Rónán's heartbeat quickened with images of the bride's swollen and stitched face. In his fear, he pushed back into the shop, locking the front door decisively behind him. He strode across the room toward the back of the shop. He was too nervous to walk along the bay, worried that the bride might emerge from the depths again whispering her solemn curses at him, so Rónán decided to walk through the alley lining the backs of the shops. As he reached the green painted door, the images of twisting vines painted on it sparked another memory in him. Years ago, on his father's birthday when Rónán was a boy, he and his mother decorated the door with twisting, flowering vines as she told him stories about his father. She told Rónán how they met as children in Ireland, how he became a sailor, and when they decided to come to America. Aislyn never seemed sad when sharing the stories, but there was always something in the tone of her voice, like she longed to create more stories to share.

Rónán entered the grassy alleyway, greeted by the muggy air. Right outside his door, sat two used wooden tubs, one was blackened on the inside from years of dyes seeping into the wood grain, the other worn but relatively clean on the inside. A tall wooden pole staked to the ground next to the tubs reminded Rónán of a skinny birch tree shorn of its branches. Running along the back wall of his shop was a line he used to hang wet clothing and fencing it all in was the garden box his father had built for his mother. A few weeds poked through the earth here and there in this garden. He definitely didn't keep it as neat as his mother had, but the plants remained the same as she left them.

Moving through the alley toward the general store on the opposite corner of his own shop, Rónán watched a stray, orange cat stretch out in a patch of sun between buildings. It lay in a patch of overgrown grass, watching the chickens that pecked at the earth outside the back door of the Duvall Family Butchery. It chittered and flicked its tail back and forth as it eyed them. Rónán made a mental note to leave some food scraps on his back steps for the little ball of fur.

He came to the back of the general store, but rather than use the rear entrance, he walked up the stone path that was sunk into the earth between the general store and the neighboring bakery. As he entered through the front door, a silvery chime caught the attention of the girl sitting on a velvet-covered stool behind the counter. Helene Hebert looked up at Rónán and smiled in greeting. Helene was a beautiful young girl with her warm chocolate eyes, dark skin, and midnight curls. Her cheeks were naturally rosy, giving her a cherubic look. Aside from Abel, Helene was the only other person in Bridewater who was around Rónán's age. She had contracted the dreadful flu that spread through the town as a child, but through treatments and whispered prayers, she managed to pull through.

"Morning," she called to him, giving him a wide smile. She didn't share her father's thick, French accent. Instead, she favored a charming Southern drawl like her mother.

"Hello, there," Rónán returned. "How are you, Helene?"

"Just fine darlin'. What're you looking for?"

Rónán nodded toward a bar of lye soap that sat high behind Helene on a shelved wall. Brushing her dark locks back over her shoulders, she climbed onto the stepstool and reached up to grasp the bar.

"Here you are, sugar," she said as she passed Rónán the bar. He thanked her, exchanging fifteen cents for the soap.

As Rónán was about to say his goodbyes, a soft tapping noise reverberated through the room. Henriette, the girl's statuesque mother, entered the main room of the general store, the beat of her shoes audible against the floor planks as she approached.

"Helene, your *papa* would like to see you. He's in his office," said Mrs. Hebert. Though Henriette had a sense of authority about her, she spoke sweetly, like a windchime blowing in the breeze, ornamenting her southern accent with the same *Franglais* her husband used.

Helene smiled a farewell toward Rónán and walked toward the back of the general store.

Mrs. Hebert and Rónán stood in silence as Helene's footfalls retreated. Henriette watched her daughter leave, ensuring that she was out of earshot, and then she turned to Rónán.

"*Chéri*," she started. "Helene is leaving for Atlanta soon, going to school. Her papa and I wanted to send her off with something special, a new dress to take with her."

The unspoken question sent a hopeful spark through Rónán. He would mend and embroider and launder until he was blue in the face, but what he really loved was creating, watching a garment take shape from a few loose threads, fabrics, and notions. He could already picture it in his head, mutton sleeves, a flowing skirt, and a cinched waist. Helene was a beautiful girl, and while she could make any outfit look exquisite, Rónán wanted to make something specially crafted to accentuate her beauty.

Henriette continued, "Nothing too fancy, and surely, we'd pay you. I'll leave the design up to the professional, but can you make it in mauve? Helene just loves it, and it looks so beautiful with her hair."

Rónán fought to keep his smile contained, bowing his head slightly to hide his sudden joy, "Yes, ma'am. It would be my pleasure."

"Ah, *merci!*" She clapped her hands together in excitement. "It is a surprise, but Helene will not leave for over a month."

In an unusual display of affection that Rónán was not used to, Mrs. Hebert embraced him and kissed him on both cheeks. When she pulled back, Rónán saw the glistening at the corner of her eyes where small tears had formed.

"I can't thank you enough, dear. You and your mother do so much for us," she said.

The unexpected mention of his mother surprised Rónán. People rarely spoke of her, at least in his presence. Her disappearance was the unspoken and assumed forgotten mystery in town. Aislyn's absence was like the family secret kept from the children until they were old enough to understand. Trying to ignore the pang in his gut, Rónán nodded his thanks to Henriette.

"I'm happy to help," he sniffed, blinking to contain the tears he could feel forming.

Without another word, not giving Henriette the chance to continue the conversation,

Rónán turned and left. As he walked back toward his shop through the long, grassy corridor between the shops, he noticed that the orange cat had slunk closer to Douglas' chicken coops. In its instinctual need to hunt, the cat chirped as it watched the chickens peck around the enclosure. The little cat provided a much-needed distraction from the memories of his mother. And despite his sadness, there was a newfound lightness in Rónán's step as he thought about the opportunity Henriette had placed before him. He knew just the fabric he would use, a soft wool.

He would need to dye it, of course, but he could do so easily. He wouldn't have time to order any fancy velvets, but he had enough lace and trimmings in the shop to make something spectacular.

As if the prospect of creating Helene's dress shot coffee directly through his veins, he no longer felt tired.

When he arrived back at his shop, in his excitement, Rónán set out to work immediately. With a bucket of water in his hand, Rónán bounded up to his room, the wooden stairs squeaking as they accepted his weight. He placed the tin bucket on the cookstove that was already ablaze. Usually, when his work called for scalding water, he would do it first thing in the morning or late at night to keep his shop from overheating, but he was too excited to wait for the evening. As he waited for the water to boil, Rónán creaked his way back down the stairs, gleefully skipping the last few.

He made his way to the bolts of fabric on the back wall behind the counter, pulling out a soft, white woolen fabric. He didn't have much left, but it was just enough to begin his work for Helene. He pulled the fabric into his face. The soft ripples caressed him, and he could smell the almost earthen aroma folded within the weave. Getting this fabric to take on a mauve hue as Henriette had requested, would not be too difficult, but it would use up the rest of his stores of purple dye. He didn't use it much anyway—a tie, handkerchief, or skirt here or there—it was one of the most laborious colors to acquire. He knew using his current stock would mean having to make another trip into the bayou soon to look for more of the lichen that produced the purple dye, but he didn't mind. He enjoyed his trips into the marshes; they were the one place where he didn't feel the eyes of Bridewater follow his every move.

Walking through the green back door, Rónán approached the two tubs. He poured a dark plum colored jar of liquid into the stained wooden basin. Carefully, using a wooden spoon so as to not color his hands, he lowered the woolen fabric, gently stirring it into the purple liquid. He threw a handful of salt into the basin and returned to his room.

With a towel to protect his hand from the heat of the tin bucket, he removed the water from the cookstove. Treading gently, he shouldered the back door open and, pouring slowly to avoid splashing himself, emptied the bucket into the second wooden washtub. Rónán always thought to himself that he would upgrade the tubs, add some sort of fire pit below them so he didn't have to haul boiling water down the stairs, but that was the kind of project he continually pushed toward another day. Pulling the bar of lye soap out of his pocket, Rónán shaved a few pieces into the lightly bubbling water. Being careful to avoid grabbing the spoon used in the dye basin, Rónán picked up a second wooden stick and stirred the hot, soapy water, sending crests of white foam bubbling to the surface.

He picked through the bag of clothes from the preacher, noting the yellowing stains blooming from the underarms and a handful of faded crimson wine stains down the front. He walked around the basin to his raised garden plot. Carefully, he ripped a handful of purple leaves from the heads of cabbage growing in the garden box. He tossed the leaves into the water and watched them float for a moment. The color secreted by the cabbage leaves was a light enough shade of purple to counteract the yellowing armpits of the preacher's clothes, whitening the fabric in the process. He stirred the preacher's clothes into the foamy, lavender pool.

For a few hours, he worked, scrubbing and applying more soap to the preacher's clothes as they soaked. Occasionally, Rónán would step to the other basin, lifting the wool from the purple depths to see if it was accepting the color. He knew it would need to sit for a while, at the very least overnight, but he was anxious and excited to begin making Helene's dress.

As the light grew dim, Rónán heard a familiar voice behind him.

"I come bearing fruit!" Abel said, with a slight bow. From the pocket of his olive-colored trousers, Abel flourished the dark brown bottle Rónán had dropped off to Douglas the day before, but now, the bottle had a green tinge, like moss on a tree. He laughed as he noticed Rónán startle at his unexpected arrival and nearly tip over the basin.

"I'm sorry if I caused that. Douglas asked me to bring this to you," Abel said as he held the bottle out with the tips of his fingers.

Rónán reached out to accept the ox gall. He felt the same slight shockwave when their fingers brushed against one another, like a static *pop* from touching a charged piece of metal.

"Thank you," Rónán said to Abel, feeling too shy to look the other boy in the eyes. A strange, warm sensation started to fill Rónán's chest, as if he had just sipped from his coffee.

"I've got somethin' else," Abel continued.

He rummaged around in his front pocket and handed the redhead a soft, rectangular package. Rónán recognized the paper wrapping from Duvall Family Butchery. He didn't buy meat often, but every now and then, the butcher would give him a scrap of salted meat, and if he were lucky, something fresh.

Rónán looked up at the young man in front of him, accepting the package. Abel was, as usual, smiling. His grin was so wide, it seemed more teeth than mouth. His big, round eyes sparkled, as if there were a joke playing at the back of his mind, but something was off. A dark, splotched, purple bruise, rivaling the color of the basin where the wool was soaking, radiated out from under Abel's left eye. Abel saw that Rónán noticed and hurriedly turned to the side, gesturing at the tub to distract him.

"What're you doin' here anyway?" He asked. As he waited for Rónán's reply, he settled on the wooden steps leading up to the back door of the tailor shop's, sprawling across the steps and leaning on his right elbow.

Rónán filled him in on his work, recalling his morning at the shopkeepers and the preacher's washing—these few sentences were the most they'd ever spoken to each other.

Then, nodding toward the wooden dowel sprouting from the ground, Abel asked, "And what's this for?"

Rather than explain, Rónán decided to show him. Gently reaching into the basin of laundry, Rónán took one of the preacher's shirts. Gripping the sleeves at the cuff in one hand and the bottom of the shirt in the other, he slung the middle over the pole. Bringing the two dangling ends in together, he began twisting the shirt. The pole stabilized the shirt in place but allowed the cloth to spiral in on itself as Rónán twisted it hand-over-hand. A few sudsy drops became a small waterfall, and the shirt was wrung free of the water it had soaked in.

"It's easier with two people, but since my ma left…" He paused for a moment, not sure what to say next. After a moment in silence, Rónán finished, "It's easier with two people, but the pole will make do."

Abel put both palms on his knees and pushed himself to a standing position with a groan. He clapped and rubbed his hands together to free whatever detritus might be hiding in the creases of his palms and said, "Well now, you've got two people. Let me help."

Rónán reacted with a grateful laugh. "Thank you," he said.

Rónán pulled another shirt from the basin. Abel, who had rolled his sleeves to his elbows, accepted one end while Rónán held the other.

"Now, you spin one way, and I'll spin the other," Rónán explained.

"I think I can manage that," Abel winked.

Holding the shirt over the wash basin, the boys twisted the cloth between them, releasing streams of water back into the basin below. As they spun the cloth, Rónán found his eyes traveling the length of cloth to Abel's hands, then up to his forearms. Abel's hands were big and slightly calloused from his work at the docks. The muscles of his forearms danced as they tightened the cloth. It reminded Rónán of the way the bay rippled smoothly on a calm day. The warmth in his gut erupted again, like taking another sip of coffee. To control his feelings he squatted and pulled another shirt from the basin.

Abel cleared his throat. As if someone had clapped right in front of his face, Rónán snapped his attention back in embarrassment, looking directly up at Abel. If he noticed Rónán's wandering eyes, he didn't let on. Instead, still smiling, Abel gestured to the second tub.

"How do you get that color, anyway? Did you bleed a pig over that tub or what?" He laughed.

Rónán shook his head. "No," he smiled shyly. "Plants."

"Plants? What do you mean plants?" Abel asked, looking bemused.

"When my ma was a girl, she learned how to use plants to dye fabrics–from her ma, I guess. And she taught me." Rónán explained, feeling a small pang speaking of his mother. He shrugged, "There are other ways to do it, I'm sure, but this is what I know."

"I ain't never seen a plant this color," Abel said, screwing his face in mock confusion.

"You sure?"

Again, Rónán chuckled. He couldn't remember the last time he had laughed like this. "I am sure."

Rónán felt the flush return to his cheeks. With a surge of bravery, he said, "I could show you. Tomorrow morning. I planned to head into the bayou to forage some plants for more dye. You could come?" He left the question hanging in the air.

"Why not?" Abel grinned, "Tomorrow's the one day I don't gotta work anyway."

Rónán nodded. After they released the tension on the shirt between them, Rónán hung it up on the clothesline behind him, letting out a sigh he hoped Abel didn't notice. They picked up another of the preacher's shirts, repeating the process.

Rónán looked again at the other boy's face. This time, his gaze lingered over Abel's bruised eye.

"You okay? What happened to you anyway?" Rónán asked, nodding to the bruise.

It was the first time that Rónán had seen Abel's face drop. Abel stayed quiet for a moment, then with a forced chuckle, he said, "Oh you know me. I'm clumsier than a drunk dog.

Accident at work. I… tripped on some boxes."

Rónán considered him for a second. "You know, my ma," a thorn of ice pricked his stomach, "she knew a bit about medicine. I could give you something for—"

SQUAWK!

Both boys snapped their necks up towards the clothesline. Sitting there, taking them both in with their dark, reflective eyes, sat two black birds. They craned their heads almost unnaturally to the side to look at the boys.

"Where'd they come from?" Abel asked no one in particular. If he were startled by the sudden interruption, he didn't show it. Rónán, however, felt a small tremor in his hands. He quickly squeezed the shirt hanging between them, hoping Abel wouldn't feel the vibrations.

"Abel?" the butcher called. From a few yards away, standing as if he were at the end of a long, dark tunnel, Douglas looked directly at his brother. "Time to get home, boy," he said in his gravelly voice.

Abel turned back to Rónán. He let go of the end of the shirt carefully so it wouldn't dip back into the wash basin. Looking down, he spoke, "I've gotta go. But I'll see you in the morning, okay?"

Rónán nodded. Without another word, Abel turned and walked toward his brother. It was getting dark, so Rónán could not see Douglas' face well, but something about the way he was shadowed against the alley, his broad shoulders framing his impressively large body, felt ominous. He tried to shake the feeling.

As Rónán watched Douglas and Abel retreat into the butchery, he saw the silhouette of the orange cat. It had taken to prowling around the foundation of one of the neighboring buildings. It jumped and waved its paws, no doubt stalking some kind of insect. Rónán pulled the salted meat from his pocket. Unwrapping it, he tore off a small chunk of the red meat and placed it on the lower step, hoping the cat would find it this evening.

Abel had helped Rónán get through a good amount of the washing, but he stayed outside to finish wringing out the clothes with the dowel before heading inside. Item by item, he released water trapped in the fabrics and hung them on the clothesline. As he worked, his thoughts turned to Abel. He racked his brain trying to recall when he had spent so much time with someone over the last decade. Nothing came to mind. Rónán kept seeing Abel's arms, the muscles tightening and rolling with every twist of fabric. He pictured Abel's hands, powerful and both hard and soft at the same time.

Though Rónán had lit a lamp at his back door, the darkness in the alleyway was creeping closer. He wanted to finish before quitting for the night, so he continued working in the dim flicker of the lamp. Then he heard the bell at his front door ring, signaling someone's entrance into his shop.

"Just a minute!" he called in through the back door.

Drying his hands on the front of his pants, he picked up the oil lamp and walked inside. He looked around, but the shop was empty. He raised his arm, using the lamp to cast flickering light into every shadowed corner.

"Hello?" he called.

When no one replied, Rónán walked around the shop again, checking for signs that someone had entered. He looked behind the counter, opened the door to the small changing room, and glanced up to the bend in the stairwell. Rónán quieted, straining to hear if there was any movement upstairs, but still, he heard nothing. He crossed to his front door, but it was still locked. He peered through the curtains, but no one waited on the other side. He swore he had heard the bell but thought perhaps his lack of sleep was catching up to him—had he imagined it?

"Hello?" He tried one more time. There was still no response.

He turned and started walking toward the back door, lamp in hand. Then, he heard a small, wet plop, as if someone had dropped a piece of cut meat on the ground. With a quick inhale, he looked behind him. No one was there. He stared directly into the corner of the room where the light of his lamp did not quite reach, but again, he saw nothing.

He turned to face the back door and looked up. Suddenly, he almost jumped out of his skin. Reflected in the small pane of glass on the painted door's window, between the soft orange flickers of the flame in his hand, he saw it.

No. He saw *her*.

As if he were looking at her through a thin, sheer fabric, Rónán saw the silhouette of the bride. She began walking slowly toward him. Her distended, graying feet made wet sounds against the wooden floor. In the wavy reflections in the glass, she looked more disjointed, her appearance more bloated, more unnatural. Her insistent, high-pitched whispering sent ice through his veins. The whispers grew louder, more urgent with each step she took closer to him.

He wanted to look away, but his eyes, now wide open in fear, were tethered to the reflection in front of him. Her hands hung awkwardly drawn together in front of her stomach, elbows at odd angles as if at least one of them were broken. The bride's wet gown clung to her decaying body. He wanted to move, to run, but it was as if his shoes were filled with mud, as if he suddenly had forgotten how to walk. He felt tears form at the corner of his eyes, but they didn't seem to want to fall. He was paralyzed. A throbbing ache started at his temples, as he watched her move closer and closer. His heart beat so fast in his chest, he could feel it pulsing in his throat.

When the bride's face was close enough to make out the crude stitches constraining her eyes and mouth, Rónán saw her lips writhing and twitching. He felt if she got closer, he would hear and understand what she was saying, but he was terrified of what it might be.

Rónán tried to scream, but his tongue felt too big and numb, like it had swollen to twice its normal size. He wanted to yell for Abel, for anyone, to come help. A cold, icy grip on his throat choked him. All that escaped his mouth were his ragged breaths, as if the bride had laced her fingers around his neck and squeezed. his guttural, fearful sobs sounded in chorus with the bride's whispers.

She was so close now that he could feel her cold, putrid breath on the back of his neck. The shock of it caused him to jump, stumbling backwards. To his horror, his arm brushed against something wet, thick with viscous slime. He had brushed against the bride. As quickly as he could, he threw himself forward, pressing his body up against the back door, making himself as small as he could. He was trapped, shaking. He wanted to create distance between him and the woman right over his shoulder. In his fear, he did the only thing he felt he could do. He shut his eyes. Pressed against the back wall, he tried to shut her out of his mind, to erase her from this place. In his head, he tried to recall a prayer his mother taught him, but to no avail. The only thing he could make sense of, that he could hear, were the sounds of the bride, louder and louder in his ears with each step she took.

He tried to press himself even closer to the wall, as if he could go right through it. The pressure caused him to bite down on his own tongue. The warm, coppery taste of blood flooded his mouth. He listened, fearful that the blood somehow alerted the woman to his weakness, scared that she could smell it in the air like a predatory shark, but he realized he couldn't hear her anymore. He tried to quiet his own breathing, to calm the heartbeat pounding in his ears to listen for the bride. He needed to be sure that the quiet of the air wasn't a trick, but he didn't hear her.

Rónán gasped, opening his eyes in a flash, and thrusting his body around to face the shop behind him. But as quickly as she had appeared, the bride was gone. He looked down. On the floor, a set of wet footprints trailed from the locked entrance of the shop to where he stood at the green painted door.

The tension holding him in place burst from his body like an explosion. Without a second thought, not bothering to finish the work he had started out back, Rónán jerked the lock of the back door closed and sprinted up the stairs. He slammed shut the door to his bedroom. He ran to the far side of the room, and, straining with the effort, he dragged his mother's vanity across the floor and it scraped and groaned against the wood in protest. He pushed the mirrored table against the door to hold it firmly closed.

Leaping, almost floating, as if the bride were waiting to grab his ankles from under the bed, he jumped onto his mattress. He sat up, hugging his knees to his chest, looking at the bedroom door. He watched the crack under the door half expecting to see the bride's feet on the other side.

This can't keep happening. Rónán thought. *But is it really happening?*

He rubbed the spot on his arm that was still cold and wet from where it made contact with the bride. That was all the confirmation he needed. With his back against the wall, Rónán rocked himself sitting up in his bed, not wanting to sleep, and waited for morning.

Chapter 4

Three sharp knocks jolted Rónán awake. He had fought sleep most of the night, but at some point, he had succumbed and dozed fitfully.

"Rónán!" Abel called in his sing-song southern drawl. "You home?"

Rónán cracked his bedroom window open. The wood groaned as he raised the window. Leaning his head out, he called down, "Just a minute!"

Abel popped his head out from under the awning, looking around to find Rónán. When they made eye contact, Abel smiled and yelled back in affirmation, "Alright then!"

Rónán hurriedly checked his appearance in the vanity that he had shoved in front of his bedroom door the night before. Puffy purple bags pillowed the underside of his eyes more pronounced after another restless night, and his cheeks were red where he'd attempted to slap himself awake throughout the night so that he looked sunburned. He quickly pulled his hair back into a messy knot low against the base of his skull. He had been in such a panic the night before, he hadn't bothered putting on sleeping clothes. The simple cotton shirt and trousers he wore now were wrinkled from sleeping, but he figured dirty clothes would suffice for today anyway. Hopping from one foot to the other, Rónán pulled on a pair of socks and stepped into his brown leather boots, the old pair that he used for trips into the bayou so as not to muddy his other boots. He looked at himself in the mirror one more time, turning his head from side to side and brushing the sleep from the inside corners of his eyes.

Rónán scraped the vanity out of the way of his door, making a mental note to return it to its correct placement later. He opened the door to the landing and bounded down the stairs.

Abel's shadow was projected onto the curtains from the morning sun rising over the bay. For a moment, Rónán stood there watching as Abel stretched his arms over his head, seeing the shadow of his shirt lift, teasingly exposing his midsection. Abel must have just woken up himself, which made Rónán feel better about his slow start.

As he watched Abel's dancing shadow, Rónán felt a flutter of excitement in his chest. He had never been accompanied on one of his foraging ventures before, let alone by someone his own age. He felt hopeful that he might finally have a friend in Bridewater.

Rónán dashed behind the front counter, collecting a gunny sack that he had made into a shoulder bag by adding two long, multicolored handles fashioned from various bits of scrap fabric. He lowered a few empty glass jars into the bag with a light clink and heaved the bag over his shoulder. He felt the glass knocking against his hip as he walked toward the front door. The brightly colored candies in the bag from Mr. Hebert caught his eye as he strode across the room.

He grabbed a handful of the sweets and chucked them into the bag.

As Rónán pulled the door inward, the bell overhead tinkled. Abel, who had been stretching while looking out over the bay, turned around with a toothy grin.

"Well, good mornin', sleepyhead!" He said, clapping Rónán on the shoulder.

Rónán blushed at the call out and couldn't help but smile. Abel always seemed to exude his own sunshine. Rónán felt something unshakably warm about Abel's presence. His hair reminded Rónán of a flaxen silk thread, his skin, a soft, supple tan leather, and his eyes, the same color as the bronze swirling pools of coffee in his mug. The only cold thing about him was the purple that surrounded his eye, now with a slight tinge of green around the edges.

"Morning," Rónán replied to him. "You ready to go?"

Abel nodded in affirmation, gesturing toward the road. "After you," he said.

The two boys set out, walking toward the old Baptist church. With Abel whistling a jaunty tune, the boys made their way past the white-steepled church. In the back of his mind, Rónán realized that in a few short hours, most of the town would be here for service. He wondered for a second about what it meant for Abel to miss church, but he decided not to ask.

They traipsed through the graveyard, winding their way between the mossy slabs marking residents past. Bridewater was practically surrounded by miles of swampland, as if it were its own island in a sea of muck. To reach the bayou they could head out in almost any direction. However, Rónán was following instructions left by his mother. When he was younger, Aislyn wouldn't allow him to join her on trips into the wetlands due to the natural predators that awaited, but she had taken the time to write out, in her tidy scrawl, the safest direction to follow to the clearing, describing several natural landmarks to look out for. The first time he tried following her instructions, he nearly got lost, but eventually he recognized the knobby set of roots she had drawn in her book and found his way back to her trail.

About a mile past the church, they entered the swamps where the red dirt of Bridewater melted into a thick, mucked earth and the sound of the waves faded into the high-pitched hum of mosquitoes. The trees around them were large, covered in dark, mossy tones of brown and green and shaded in a graying Spanish moss. The trees gave the impression of giants hunched over, wispy hair cascading down. As the boys walked deeper into the bayou, the trees around them grew thicker, the ground wetter, and the light more dim under the tangled canopy.

On this Sunday morning, the heat and the humidity amplified by the dank wetness of the swamp felt heavy. Walking at Rónán's side, Abel rolled up his sleeves. His cotton shirt, once white in color, had assumed a soft, primrose yellow from years of work and sweat. It was purposefully large, allowing for both easy movement and ventilation in the Louisiana heat. Rónán glanced over at Abel, noticing his sun-kissed forearms with fine, golden hair that had waved in the breeze. Rónán's mind wandered to the previous evening. He remembered the muscle rippling beneath the surface of Abel's skin, and his cheeks flushed. The sweat racing down his spine cooled him, but when he saw that Abel had noticed, he felt embarrassed.

"It sure is hot, ain't it?" Abel said, breaking the silence.

Rónán shifted his attention and cleared his throat. "Sure is," he said. "I'm glad we got started early."

For another quarter hour, the boys padded carefully through the wet earth into the swamp. There was something otherworldly about the bayou. Rotting mangrove trees hung menacingly over the murky, scummy waters, their roots carpeting the musty earth. In the light cast between the trees, fog curled over the green waters. A faint earthy smell filled their nostrils from the briny decay around them, but there was life here, humming everywhere. The growling of gators, the croaking of bullfrogs, and the buzzing of insects vibrated around them.

"Look there," Abel said, pointing to a branch ahead of them. Hanging, like a discarded piece of rope, was a snake with curling patterns of green wrapping its body.

"A water snake," Rónán said, examining the creature. It hung off the forked end of a gnarled branch like it was lounging in a hammock. "It's harmless—at least to us."

Abel looked amused, "How do you know that?"

Rónán blushed. Scratching the back of his neck with his hand, he replied, "Ma's books."

"Huh," Abel said with a smile. "What about that?" He pointed up to a preening bird in another tree. The bird's plumage was shiny and black besides the bright red caps at the point where its wings met its body.

Rónán stifled a smile, "Guess."

Abel squinted up at the bird, "A... crow?" he questioned.

"Not quite," Rónán laughed, and then, as if it were obvious, he said, "It's a red-winged blackbird."

Abel's eyebrows shot up, disappearing beneath the wavy fringe that hung on his forehead. He pursed his lips together, slowly nodding, "Well, that certainly is a creative name.

It's a beautiful bird."

The way he said the last sentence in a tone of exaggerated mock appreciation made Rónán laugh again. He looked back at Abel, taking in his face, and blushed.

"It certainly is," Rónán agreed.

As they pushed on mucking through the swamp, they continued this game with Abel spotting an animal, and Rónán naming it when he could. When they came across a large, moss-covered rock, Rónán looked to his right, finding a familiar tree. His mother had written about and sketched this crooked tree, bent so drastically to the side, it looked as if it had been restrained and forced to grow at this odd angle. Rónán knew that this tree marked the path they would need to take next.

"Here," Rónán said, gesturing to the tree. "You might want to take your shoes off."

When he saw Abel's confused face, Rónán continued, "You'll never get rid of the mud if you don't."

With that, Rónán took off his boots, neatly rolling up his pant legs and sleeves. He knotted the ends of the boot laces together and slung them over the same shoulder supporting the bag of supplies. Abel followed suit, though his clumsy, pushed up sleeves and pants weren't as neatly rolled as Rónán's. His boots, which were fashioned of light brown leather made soft by years of use, hung lazily over his right shoulder.

Carefully, Rónán pulled back a branch that hung low on the tree, gesturing for Abel to walk underneath it. As he ducked under, Rónán followed him through, his bare feel squelching into the slimy mud below.

"I don't recall signing up for all this dirty work," Abel laughed, though Rónán had the distinct impression that dirty work had never bothered Abel a day in his life.

Rolling his eyes and taking the lead, Rónán replied, "The clearing is just up ahead."

The area they moved into now had a slight slope. As the boys trekked through the mud, they placed their feet carefully, testing with one foot so as to not slip before moving their full weight to the leg. Their clothes became sticky with sweat, clinging to them in the moist air, weighing them down. After another quarter hour of wading through the mud and slapping mosquitoes, Rónán saw the clearing up ahead.

"There." He pointed to a patch of sunlight that stood out in the gloom around them.

The boys picked their way over to the clearing. The small glade they entered was brighter than the rest of the bayou. The canopy overhead was sparse, allowing more sunlight to stream through the treetops. In the center was a small, murky pool that seemed to be connected to the rest of the swamp by a stream. The waters spiraled and curled around an enclosure of trees and stones. Everything was covered in something that resembled mold. Rónán scooped up a handful of the leaflike fungus, holding it out to show Abel.

"My ma called this crotal," Rónán explained, rotating the palmful of the bloom to show Abel. "She taught me how to use it to make dye for the shop. When it soaks in—" he didn't want to say urine—"when it soaks in a liquid for a few weeks, it makes a deep purple color."

"Like the tub you're using for Helene's dress?" Abel asked.

"Yes, just like that."

"I don't see how this ugly thing," Abel said, palming his own handful of the soft algae from the base of the trees in the clearing, "will make anything close to that purple you showed me yesterday."

"It's true!" Rónán said, seeing the mischievous grin on Abel's face. "My ma taught me.

We've always done it."

Rónán removed the glass jars from his bag, lining them neatly on a flat section of rock in the clearing. He placed his handful of lichen into one of the jars and continued scooping it up by the handful.

Abel still looked at Rónán with a curious look.

"So, what?" he began, "You put this *gunk* in a jar, scoop some water up from the bay, and *poof!* purple dye?" Abel mimicked a small explosion with his free hand.

Rónán considered Abel for a second, suddenly embarrassed again. "Not exactly. I don't use water from the bay…" his words trailed off.

"Then what do you use?" Abel asked.

"Well," Rónán looked down at his own hands, "if you must know, the crotal soaks in jars of… jars of urine, and—"

"Urine?!" Abel threw his head back in a laugh. "And do the ladies of Bridewater know you are just pissing all over their clothes? Does Helene know?"

"It's not that simple," Rónán attempted to explain himself. "I don't *piss all over their clothes.* It can't be fresh urine. It has to sit for a week or two, and…"

This made Abel laugh even more. Rónán was suddenly flustered, and too aware of himself to continue.

"Oh, come on!" Abel said, clapping Rónán on the shoulder. "I'm just playin' with you, and there's a few ladies whose clothes I'd love to piss on myself. Remember that old hag, Mrs. Francis? Now, she's a real bitch."

Rónán sighed, relieved by the way the conversation had shifted, and he finally laughed, himself.

"What's wrong with Mrs. Francis?" He asked.

Ancient Mrs. Francis was the widow of the man who owned the docks. Naturally, she and her husband were the wealthiest people in Bridewater Bay, or at least as wealthy as someone who lives in Bridewater can be. Rónán hadn't interacted with her much, but she was still pleasant enough toward him.

"What isn't wrong with her?" Abel replied.

Rónán shook his head and laughed. Feeling lighter, the two boys continued working, filling the jars one-by-one.

"And what's this one?" Abel asked.

Rónán looked up to see him approaching a tall plant with branching umbrellas of small white flowers. The leaves of the plant were bright green, and the thick, hollow stems were mottled with green and purple stripes.

"Don't touch that one!" Rónán said, causing Abel to pull his hand back like he received a static shock. "That is water hemlock—the most poisonous thing you'll find out here besides snakes and spiders."

"Poisonous?" Abel asked, looking at the plant up and down. "But it just looks like a bunch of flowers."

"Bunch of flowers or not, you mess with that too much, and you'll be sweating and spitting and itching. It can even kill you. Ma warned me about that one, too," Rónán said.

Abel raised both of his hands in a mocking gesture of horror, "Duly noted."

Rónán shook his head again and laughed. The sun overheard moved toward the middle of the sky, making the clearing hotter and brighter. The longer they worked, the more damp their shirts grew with sweat darkening in the middle of their backs.

"It's hotter than the devil out here," Abel exclaimed. Button-by-button, he unfastened his shirt and allowed it to fall open, revealing his abdomen, gleaming with fine, golden hairs and sweat. Rónán glanced at him, his eyes lingering on the boy's navel, and slowly panning down the trail of hair leading to his beltline.

As if slapped, Rónán realized what he was doing. He cleared his throat and shifted his gaze in another direction.

Intentionally not looking at Abel, he said, "It sure is."

Abel wiped away a bead of sweat running down his forehead with the back of his hand.

"I've got an idea," he said. "You showed me this place. How about I show you my place? We can cool off before heading back to the bay."

Carefully, Rónán returned the now full jars back into his burlap sack. Slinging the bag and his shoes back over his shoulder, Rónán said, "Lead the way."

They traipsed back through the muck and the underbrush, until they reached a blackwater river that ran through the swamps.

"Up this way," Abel said, gesturing to the river made dark by decades of decay. "Follow me."

Rónán followed behind Abel. Abel's open shirt flowed like a cape in a wake behind him, and the midday sun cast light through it, causing the shirt to glow soft yellow like a paper lantern. The shadow of Abel's torso was silhouetted against the backdrop of the shirt. Rónán took in the shape of Abel's body, illuminated by the afternoon sun. He felt a warmth in his gut that had nothing to do with the heat of the day.

"It's just ahead now," Abel said.

As they followed the meandering blackwater, the trees thinned out slightly and the ground became less muddy and more lushly green. When they came to a line of tall grass and bushes, Abel said, "just through here."

He started pushing his way into the overgrowth. Then, emphasizing the word with two syllables in his Southern style, Abel yelped, "Shee-it."

Rónán looked up to see that Abel's shirt had snagged in the maw of a thorn bush he didn't recognize. A large hole now exposed Abel's shoulder. Through the hole, Rónán saw a thin, bloody scratch deep red against his tanned skin.

As Abel wiggled his shirt free and laughed again, "Good thing I know a tailor."

Abel continued leading the way through the brush. Rónán found his eyes examining the bright red line of blood running down the hard muscle of Abel's shoulder. His eyes washed over the divots of Abel's shoulder blades, and he found himself admiring the natural, chiseled muscle in Abel's back. He felt his heart leap.

"Here we are," Abel announced, pushing through the last web of undergrowth. "The oasis of Bridewater Bay."

He gestured to the crescent moon shaped pool before them. It was indeed an oasis. The water was the clearest Rónán had ever seen near Bridewater, and it was surrounded by lush, flowering plants. A large ash tree leaned over the space. Besides the necessary patches of shade that the tree provided, several pockets of beaming sunlight brightened the greenery. Near the edge of the water was a large, flat rock. It almost reminded Rónán of the docks across from his shop.

"Wow," Rónán said taking in the sight.

"Douglas and I used to come here as kids. And our daddy before that. I used to be convinced we were the only people in Bridewater who knew about it. Daddy called it an oxbow or somethin' like that."

Abel turned around to face Rónán with his hands on his hips and a proud smile beaming on his face. Rónán again found himself noticing the open shirt. He wanted to look away, but he couldn't. Something about his friend standing before him was captivating. Looking at Abel made his breath quicken, and a cool bead of sweat streaked down his temple.

"Well, what're we waitin' for?" Abel grinned, pushing his sweat slick hair back from his face.

Standing on the flat rock near the edge of the pool, Abel tossed his shoes to the side. His shirt, already unbuttoned, came off quickly. Then, unknotting the twine that belted his pants, Abel dropped his trousers to the ground, kicking them off. Without looking back, Abel, now nude, sprinted and dove into the water with a wild laugh.

Pushing up from the clear depths, Abel looked at Rónán. Sending a spray of cold water at him, he yelled, "Get in, tailor!"

Rónán debated whether it would be weirder to join his friend or ignore him but ultimately started removing his clothes. When he shuffled out of his pants, he became hyper aware of every inch of his body. He crossed his hands in front of himself, cupping himself in modesty. In his mind he could see every hair, every freckle, and every blemish showing against his white skin.

With this new self-consciousness, he felt the familiar trembling in his hands.

"You'll have to get in fast," Abel called to him. "Or it'll be too cold."

Rónán again weighed what was worse, jumping in or standing by the edge. He decided he had to go for it. So he dove into the water, sending ripples out in every direction. Abel turned his head to avoid the splash and laughed. When Rónán resurfaced, he could taste the salty sweet mixture of his sweat and the pool water trickling down his face into his mouth.

Abel said, "See it's not so bad. Just look out for the leeches."

When Rónán reacted in fear and disgust, Abel threw his head back in laughter again, reminding Rónán of the call of a seagull.

"I'm only joking," he said. "I wish you could see your face."

Rónán splashed his friend playfully, grinning.

"Oh, look there," Abel said, pointing over Rónán's shoulder. Rónán just looked at him for a moment, squinting his eyes in suspension.

"No, really," Abel continued. "Look!"

With a sideways glance at Abel, Rónán slowly turned his head to look behind him.

Just above a peach-pink flower, a shiny, emerald green hummingbird, accented in ruby and white, hovered in place. The way the sunlight hit the bird made it shine even more brilliantly.

Rónán could barely hear the soft droning of its wings.

"That's good luck," Rónán said. "At least, that's what Ma always said." She had told him something else about the beautiful bird, but he couldn't recall exactly what. The boys watched it for a moment as it flitted from bud to bud, both appreciating the natural beauty of its movements. "You sure do know a lot about birds," Abel joked. His voice cut into the soft beating of the hummingbird's wings. "A bird expert, swamp plant specialist, and master tailor—what can't you do?"

Rónán nodded, his memory bringing up images of his mother. Abel seemed to notice this retreat into his own head, so he let the question hang between them, and kicked back to float in the sunlight. They drifted in the water like floating lilies, allowing the cool water to soothe their bodies. After a while, Abel kicked his way to the edge of the pool and pulled himself onto the flat rock. There, he stood, yawning and stretching, his face tilted up to the sky.

Rónán observed Abel as he stretched and arched his back, his muscles on full display.

There was a strange, almost uncomfortable, feeling in the pit of Rónán's stomach. It was something he couldn't immediately place, something he couldn't recognize. He grasped for meaning inside his head, but nothing came. All he knew was that he wanted to look at Abel, to take him in. His friend was beautiful—his golden skin, slick and wet, shining in the late afternoon sun, his sandy hair falling gently across his face in waterlogged curls. The gold and green of the sunlight through the trees behind him framed him, like a regal statue. Rónán's eyes wandered over every part of his friend's body, from the top of his head to his shoulders, to his chest and the soft pink of his nipples, to the light golden hair that covered his chest and abdomen. Slowly Rónán's eyes traveled down and stopped momentarily on Abel's penis.

Something new stirred inside him. And suddenly, he felt wrong, ashamed. He quickly averted his eyes.

Still fully nude, Abel leaned down and picked up both sets of clothes. He knelt at the edge of the pool and dipped their clothes in the water, swirling them around to free the caked-on dirt and sweat. He laid Rónán's clothes out flat on the rock to dry. His own pants he rolled into a clumsy pillow. Plopping the pillow on the ground, he laid his head down, stretching out to feel the sun, sunbathing like a turtle on a log. Then, he draped one arm of his shirt over his face, shading him from the sun.

He sighed, "I love coming here."

In less than a minute, his breathing deepened, and Rónán realized that Abel had fallen asleep. Rónán used this opportunity to quickly dress himself. He sat on the flat rock, facing away from Abel, his back against the mossy ash tree. For a moment, he watched the sun sink farther into the sky, fading from bright white to a soft dandelion mist. He leaned his head back, closed his eyes, and he, too, drifted to sleep.

*　*　*

SQUAWK!
With a start, Rónán's eyes shot open. He didn't know how long it had been, but the pink in the sky and the purple haze around him told him that night was falling. On a branch above him, the three blackbirds that had awakened him looked down. Their

eyes seemed to burrow into Rónán's skull. There was something unsettling about their unblinking, unemotional gaze.

Turning, Rónán nudged Abel's shoulder. With a start Abel woke up. As he came to his senses, he yawned and pulled the sleeve from his face.

"It's getting late," Abel observed. "I'm sorry I fell asleep on you."

"I slept, too," Rónán said. "Honestly, I haven't been sleeping well lately."

"That would explain this morning," Abel said, referencing Rónán's late start to the day.

He faced his friend and laughed, "You look almost as bruised as me."

Rónán touched the bags under his eyes with his fingertips, hyper aware of their prominence on his face. But Abel seemed to pay no more attention to them.

As Abel began pulling on his clothes, he frowned and looked again at his friend, "Why can't you sleep?"

Rónán sat silent for a second, not sure how to explain. Then, he said, "It's a long story." Abel chuckled. "Well, we have a hike back to Bridewater, and I like long stories."

Rónán considered for a second, let out a sigh, and then told him. "I saw someone."

Abel looked at him expectantly, and with an exaggerated wave of his hand coaxed

"*...and?*"

"And it scared me. There was just someone walking down the road late at night, and it caught me off guard. That's all."

"Oh, don't tell me," Abel smiled, "you saw *the bride*?" He accented the last words with a mocking, haunting tone.

Abel's smile faded as he noticed Rónán averting his gaze. Abel furrowed his brow. "Did you really?"

When Rónán didn't reply, Abel continued, his voice sounding unusually serious. "You know the story of the bride of Bridewater right?"

Rónán nodded.

"My daddy used to tell the story to me and Douglas to scare us. But it happened a long time ago. Before my daddy, before even my granddaddy came here," Abel said. Shifting his weight forward, looking directly at Rónán, he continued. "Did you know the town was once called Brinewater?"

"No. I didn't."

"The water in the bay was so thick with salt that it was said nothing—no plant, no fish— could live there. That's why the people had to build the docks. There was no way to support themselves by fishing alone, so they had to rely on shipping. Anyway, before the docks were built, only a handful of people lived in Brinewater Bay. One of those people was the bride. She was said to be a tall, slender, beautiful woman—the most beautiful in the village."

As Abel spoke, Rónán saw her image emerging out of the depths of the back of his mind, slowly becoming clearer. The graying, bloated, dripping woman he had seen every night. Her dark hair, plastered to her bruised, discolored face.

"It was said that on the night before her wedding, she caught her fiancé kissing another woman. She was so distraught that on that same night, she put on her wedding gown, tied her own arms together, and walked into the water, drowning herself. People say that at night she still swims up from the bay and walks around town crying for her husband."

In his mind, Rónán saw the stitches that held her eyes and mouth together, heard her whispers that bled through the corners of her mouth. Was she really crying for her husband? Did she think Rónán was her husband? He shivered, not from the darkness settling around them.

"I, for one, hope she finds him," Abel laughed. "Besides, have you ever noticed how almost no one seems to get married in Bridewater?"

Rónán had of course raised the hems of gowns and let out the seams of jackets enough times to know that most people in town went to the church in Pine Hollow a few miles outside of town when they were getting married, but he had never given it much thought.

In Rónán's silence, Abel continued, "They say the bride curses any marriage that happens in view of the bay, though that didn't stop Douglas and Clementine. I think they were the first couple to get married in the Baptist church in fifty years." Abel's face darkened, a memory floating behind his eyes. He continued, "Clementine is scared of her own shadow. She won't even go to the general store alone, but ancient curses be damned, I guess?"

Abel looked up. Noticing the pained look on Rónán's face, seeing the fear, Abel reassured him. "It's okay. It's just a story—a superstition."

Rónán forced the bride out of his mind and looked at Abel. "I know," he said. "It must've been a bad dream or something."

He wiped a tear from the corner of his eye. They sat in an awkward silence for a moment, neither sure what to say to the other. The story of the bride hung in the air between them.

"We better get heading back," Abel said. "Douglas won't be happy with how long I've been gone today, and knowing him, he's probably still slurring from the communion wine."

Rónán nodded. The boys began to gather their things. In the shallows of the pool, Rónán noticed a green, flowering plant breaking through the surface. The thick stems and broad leaves were intertwined with delicate white flowers, bright yellow puffs in their centers. He gripped a few stalks and yanked a few bulbous plants free.

"Swamp potato," he said to Abel's confused look. "It's a bit early in the season for them, but…" he shrugged, not wanting to acknowledge that he needed something to eat.

"See," Abel said as he dressed himself. He winked at Rónán, "Swamp plant specialist."

When they were clothed and booted, they began their walk back toward Bridewater, following the winding blackwater river to the outskirts of town. Twilight blanketed them as they walked back. The calls of nocturnal birds and bullfrogs provided a natural soundtrack to their return. They mostly remained silent, but every now and then, Abel hummed a melody to himself.

Eventually, they passed back by the church and crossed the road into the heart of town.

As they came to the tailor shop, Rónán turned to Abel. "Thank you for coming with me today. Come by the shop tomorrow, and I'll fix your shirt," He nodded toward the hole on Abel's shoulder.

Abel raised his shoulder, angling his face a quarter turn to see the hole. He laughed, "Of course. I'll go with you anytime."

Rónán felt a soft percussive beat in his stomach.

"Goodnight," he said to Abel.

"Night," Abel replied, flashing his teeth in one last smile.

Rónán watched him walk toward the butcher shop. When Abel dissolved into the darkness of the night, Rónán turned and entered his shop.

Though he had napped at the pond earlier that day, he felt exhausted, the sun and heat having burnt the energy out of him. He sorted the contents of his shoulder bag, organizing the jars of crotal on a lower shelf. Gripping the flowering stems of the swamp potatoes in his hand, he bounded upstairs to his bedroom, hearing the familiar creak.

In the room, his mother's vanity still sat crooked near the door. He thought for a moment about leaving it there that night, even pushing it again in front of his bedroom door, but instead; he slid it back to the other side of the room to the corner where it usually sat. He slid the stool back to its place in front of the vanity and tossed the shock of dirty potatoes onto the desk.

Rónán looked at himself in the mirror. His face was still red, but this time it really was sun-kissed from the day. Though he wasn't quite sunburned, any amount of pigment stood out against his milky white flesh. He removed his shirt. As it slid down his body, revealing more of his bare skin, flickers of Abel danced in his mind. Where Abel was golden, tanned, and chiseled, Rónán was cool, white, and soft. His mind's eye lingered over the muscles of Abel's body. He thought of Abel's hands, calloused and powerful. He could see every vein that ran along their backs. He imagined those hands sliding over Abel's torso, across the hair below his navel, until they reached below the belt line.

Rónán closed his eyes to block out all other thoughts. As he replayed these images, he found his own hands moving lower on his body. With an ecstatic gasp, Rónán gripped his own cock, sending a shock of pleasure through his body. He continued thinking about Abel, stroking himself in quick, even movements. His heart beat fast. He was sure he would see it pumping in his chest.

His breath grew deeper and quickened. He felt a sense of urgency now as his chest and stomach grew warm. As he felt himself coming to a release, he opened his eyes and saw himself in the mirror. Suddenly, he was deluged with shame and the images of Abel washed from his mind as if someone had dumped a bucket of ice-cold water on his head.

Rónán felt sick to his stomach. In his embarrassment, he purposefully and quickly dressed himself, this time putting on his nightshirt.

All of these feelings were new. When Rónán thought of Abel, he felt warm. He felt like he had a friend for the first time in his entire life in Bridewater. But when that sunlight of warmth became too bright, he felt ashamed, disgusted by the thoughts that played out in his mind.

In this moment of vulnerability, Rónán missed his mother. Through the shame and the guilt and even the longing, he just wanted someone to tell, someone to talk to. Someone who could hug him and say everything would be all right.

Rónán crossed the room to his bed. Throwing back the covers, he dropped onto the down mattress. The only thing that could quiet his mind now was sleep. He dropped his head back onto his pillow and closed his eyes. He heard the water lapping the bay and the nocturnal music of wild animals wafting into his room. The hum of these noises combined with his tiredness from lack of sleep caught up to him. Before he knew it, Rónán was asleep.

Thunk.

Snorting, Rónán awoke.

Thunk.

He opened his eyes, blinking into the darkness.

Thunk.

Rónán jerked himself upright in his bed. "Hello?" He called into the darkness.

He recognized a familiar sound—the dry groan of the wooden stairs. His heart was pounding again.

"Is someone there?" He called, his voice quivering like the flame of a candle, but there was no reply.

His room was eerily silent. All Rónán could hear was the creaking of the steps and the beating of his heart. The footfalls grew closer, closer, until they stopped right outside his bedroom door.

Wide-eyed and shaking Rónán watched his bedroom door crack ever so slightly open, the hinges caterwauling. Behind the open door blackness filled the landing at the top of the stairs.

Rónán was crying now, a quiet, spasmodic type of cry. He could not remove his eyes from the void beyond the crack in his doorway.

"H-hello?" he tried one more time, hoping against all hope that no one would respond.

But respond she did. The bride's incessant whispered chanting for her husband, filled the empty spaces of his room. The noise suffocated him, like his room was slowly filling with murky, silty swamp water.

His hands shaking, Rónán reached to his right, pulling a single match from the surface of his vanity table. Not taking his eyes from the door, Rónán struck the match against his bed frame. It lit with a sulfuric hiss. There was a small burst of light, not enough to illuminate his entire room but enough to provide momentary comfort.

Rónán heard another creak. The door slowly pushed farther into his room. The whispering became louder, more insistent. The bride was desperate to be heard. Then, as if a snake were slithering along the door frame, he saw a blackened finger curl around the edge of the door, its cracked nail seeking the handle.

Rónán was paralyzed with fear. The flame of the match began to lick at his fingertips, but Rónán couldn't feel his skin singe as the flame died at the end of the matchstick. Again, darkness covered him. Without the flickering flame of the match, the room became even darker as his eyes struggled to adjust. He couldn't make out any shape in the blackness, but he could still hear her.

The bride's hissing sounded like a snake hiding in the grass.

The hinges of the door squealed as it creaked farther open. The floorboards joined the chorus with a wet, padding noise. Though he couldn't see her, Rónán heard the bride's steps and whispers grow louder in the darkness.

He fumbled for another match and tried to strike it, but his grip was weak, and the flame didn't take.

The bride moved closer.

He breathed out in a shudder, feeling tears streak down his face. He tried again to strike the match.

The whispers grew more insistent. Her shuffling steps moved quicker.

He struck the match a third time. This time it took, and the momentary flash illuminated the emptiness in front of him. Rónán stared into this space for a moment, begging his eyes to adjust. He used the match to light the oil lamp that sat beside his bed. In the new cascade of light, he looked around. *The bride was not there.* He listened closely, but he no longer heard her whispering.

He picked up the lamp, desperately trying to cast light into every darkened corner, but the woman was gone. There was just enough light to see that his bedroom door stood wide open. He stared into the landing, scared that something might emerge from the darkness just beyond the reach of the flame. He looked down. There on the floor was a set of muddy footprints, materializing in the abysmal blackness.

Feeling a rush of bravery, Rónán jumped to his feet and ran to the door, pushing it closed with an emphatic click. He stood there for a moment, back against the door, his chest heaving in anxious breaths. He looked down again at the wet prints. They stopped right at the edge of his bed. They did not retreat or lead anywhere else, as if the drowned bride had just stood at his bed and then vanished.

Keeping his lamp lit, the price of oil be damned, Rónán climbed back into bed. He tried to sleep, but he could not quiet the whispers reverberating in his mind. He kept seeing the creeping fingers of the woman spider their way around the edge of his doorway. He kept hearing the squeaking hinges and the creaking floorboards as she moved toward him. And he kept thinking about the urgency with which the woman continued to whisper her gurgled message through the small slit at the edge of her mouth.

Rónán sat in bed, staring at the ceiling, until the darkness faded into the bright orange of the morning. When he heard the roosters calling, he pushed himself out of bed and down the stairs to his shop.

Chapter 5

Rónán looked around the empty shop. Bolts of fabric leaned lazily in various nooks around the store, and tendrils of threads wandered the floor like the creeping vines that lined the bayou beds. The state of the shop seemed to mirror the chaos in his mind, and his head ached with a dull throb of tiredness he wasn't used to feeling. His movements felt slower, forced. The sunshine memory of his trip to the swamp with Abel could not burn through the fog of his exhaustion

Yawning, he strode across the shop to open the drapes that blocked out the morning. As he slid them back, he peered out over the waters of Bridewater Bay. The sun was still low in the sky, and the hum of life had not yet returned to the docks. Even in his still anxious state, there was a sense of peace. He watched the water for a moment, seeing a gull dip swiftly out of the sky to fish something out of the shallows.

As quickly as the seabird dove toward the water, Rónán felt sadness wash over him. So much about their trip to the swamps yesterday reminded him of his mother, from the way he followed her directions to the hollow clearing with the lichens to the way he was able to recall the plants and wildlife that hummed around him. Aislyn's flaming hair illuminated the crevices of his mind. Her soft, blue eyes sparkled like the clear, cool waters of the oxbow. Even Aislyn's smile—oh her smile!—warmed the cold of his sadness.

Some days, it was hard to accept that his mother was truly gone. It had been a decade since she left, but some days, the anguish felt just as real, just as painful, as it had the first night he had tried to sleep without her bedtime whispers and goodnight kisses. That night he'd been a child. His bedroom had felt exceptionally large and himself infinitely small. He had felt like a frightened child exploring a stumbled-upon cave for the first time, its caverns echoing with hollow drops of salty water, certain that creatures waited around each corner to pounce when he least expected them.

For what seemed like days after his mother disappeared, he had lain in bed, hugging the stuffed seal Aislyn had made him. In bed, he hummed songs to himself that his mother had brought with her from Ireland. When all his tears had dried and the hunger strumming in his stomach became too much to bear, he finally rose. He wiped his face, made his bed, and descended into the shop. Seeing his mother's unfinished work sitting in wait, he did the only thing he knew how to do, the only thing that would calm the trembling that had begun in his hands: he got to work.

Nearly two weeks later, the first person to knock on his door had been Douglas Duvall, Abel's brother. He came to pick up a pair of laundered and patched aprons. He peered over Rónán's head into the distant corners of the shop trying to confirm the town's suspicions and accepted the folded cloth. He seemed content to leave the boy as he was, and the rest of Bridewater followed suit. And thus, Rónán had remained alone for the next decade. Day-after-day, night-after-night, and year-after-year, Rónán worked, only waiting, hoping for the bell to chime and for him to turn and see his mother walking in the door. He wouldn't even question her; he would just be grateful that she returned. But that day never came.

In the present, Rónán's consciousness shifted to his view of the bay. Familiar, yawning faces rubbed their eyes and moved past his windows on their way to the docks, signaling that life had begun to stir in Bridewater Bay. One of those faces belonged to Abel. His sandy, tousled head bobbed among the other men who moved toward the docks. Rónán's eyes found the horizontal tear in Abel's shirt that still exposed one muscled shoulder. A flutter in his chest, like that shining green hummingbird they'd watched the day before made him move his gaze away from Abel. A wave of shame tried to drown the ruby-throated bird that beat against his heart. Even alone, Rónán was ashamed recalling how he touched himself while thinking of his friend, the way he sought pleasure imagining Abel's body. His eyebrows knit together, and, with his head in his hands, he tried to rub away the hot embarrassment that surged beneath his skin. He felt his hands begin to shake.

Rónán turned toward the door at the back of his shop that led to the grassy alleyway, between his building and others. Pulling the door open, the wet, stifling air of the bay blanketed him. The preacher's clothing still hung on the clothesline, moving lazily in the salty breeze. He had the uncomfortable impression of a crowd of churchgoers standing behind his shop, watching him work. Rónán removed each item of clothing one at a time, carefully folding the pieces and palming away any stubborn wrinkles that remained. When each of the preacher's garments was neatly folded and stacked, Rónán took them inside the shop and laid them on the front counter.

As he did so, he glanced towards the docks again. Like a bee to a flower, his eyes immediately found Abel. Even from a distance, he noted the power with which Abel muscled the crates around at the docks. It looked effortless, like for him brawning shipping wares was as easy as steering a needle and thread was for Rónán.

Shaking himself from his trance, Rónán moved toward the rear of the shop, reaching down with a grunt to pull the plug from the washing basin and watching the soapy dregs moisten the yellowing grass. Then, approaching the second basin, he grabbed the long wooden spoon and lifted the woolen fabric from the purple dye. The fabric drank up the dusty mauve color. Happy with the progress, he removed the fabric. He carefully handled the dripping fabric to avoid staining his clothing and hung it on the line to dry. Once it was dry, he would wash it again and begin creating the dress for Helene.

The prospect of making Helene's gown excited him. He loved the opportunity to make something new. He returned to his countertop, pulling out a pencil and one of his mother's old books. Helene was a beautiful girl; her face held the kindness of her father while she was statuesque and graceful like her mother. Her dark, silken curls always seemed to shine and flowed as she walked even when there was no summer breeze. Her rosy skin was like a rich, sweet chocolate. Rónán knew anything he made would be made more beautiful by the girl, but he wanted to create something memorable in its own right, no matter its wearer. He wanted to make something his mother would be proud of.

This realization startled him, but this time, it didn't make him sad. Rónán wasn't fully sure how to describe the feeling, but it remained. It reminded him of when his mother would tap on his right shoulder only to quickly duck around to his left. He would turn and laugh, expecting to see her, but the space behind him remained empty. He'd feel a brief flash of confusion soon replaced by giggles as she began tickling him from the other side. He would smile and melt with delight.

Only, this time, she didn't reappear.

Rónán began to sketch. Meticulously, he drew out the pieces of the dress that he knew would make it special—the leg-o-mutton sleeves, the band collar, the ruffled skirt, and the cinched waist. He imagined each fitting Helene's body perfectly.

Picturing Helene's curves, Rónán didn't feel the same tender warmth he did when looking at Abel's muscled body. He thought of her beautiful face with her plump, shining lips. He pictured her thin waist and her wide hips. He even imagined her round breasts—all the parts of her he knew he was supposed to want— and he felt wrong, broken. Helene was a stunningly beautiful and kind young woman, but Rónán felt no hummingbirds flapping against his ribcage, no warmth rising through his chest. He didn't want her the way he wanted Abel. The tension in his gut traveled upward to form a knot in his throat and he felt ashamed.

Rónán pushed the sketchbook away from him. He glanced outside the large panes of glass and could see the sunlight melting into twilight. He hadn't realized how much time he spent sketching, but looking around the floor, he saw crumpled pieces of paper that spoke to how many times he started his sketch over. Rónán was not usually a perfectionist, but he was in this moment.

A small grumble announced his hunger. Rónán hadn't eaten all day. He remembered the meat that Abel had delivered, so he decided to make something to eat. The one food his mother always seemed to make, no matter how often Rónán pretended he didn't like it and no matter how hot the day, was a kind of stew. Usually, it was filled with slices of swamp potato, pieces of wild carrot, and chopped herbs from Aislyn's garden. If they were lucky, Aislyn would spoon in cuts of lamb or beef, boiling the whole pot together until everything was tender.

Rónán returned to his room for the bundle of swamp potatoes on his vanity and set out to make his mother's stew. He didn't have any carrots, and he wasn't sure which of his mother's herbs to throw into the pot, but he tossed a generous helping of rosemary and salt into the pot with the vegetables, hoping it would be an edible semblance of his mother's cooking. The potatoes were still early in season, but he figured if he boiled them long enough, they would still taste good. He unwrapped the parcel of meat from Douglas and found a fatty piece of beef, sliced it into thin, even strips, and plopped it into the softly bubbling pot.

Through swirling wisps of steam Rónán watched the pot's contents babble. The soft sounds of the rumbling stew sent his memory trailing to his mother again. How many times had he sat on the floor as she hummed and cooked, telling him stories of her girlhood back in Ireland? How many times did they share a bowl of stew over a piece of grainy, fresh-baked bread? Sadness amplified his hunger pains.

A sharp, metallic ringing suddenly called his attention back to his surroundings. Rónán felt sick as he remembered the other night—the front door's bell and the ghost bride's appearance. Rónán's hands shook, and he tensed as he listened for movement in the floor below.

"Hello?" Abel called. "I'm here to see a tailor about a shirt."

His tightness melted away. He rose to his feet and creaked down the steps. Abel grinned up at him in his warm, toothy way.

"Well, there he is," Abel called playfully, "The tailor of Bridewater Bay!"

Rónán laughed. "I was just making supper upstairs. If you can wait a moment, I can fix that hole for you." He gestured toward the tear in Abel's shoulder.

"I don't mind waiting," Abel replied. "Not like I have many other options. I sure do love Clementine, but she's never quite picked up the fine art of sewing. At least not like you."

Rónán blushed. "I'll grab a needle and thread, and we can head upstairs," Rónán tilted his chin towards the stairs.

"After you," Abel smiled back at him.

They walked up the stairs to Rónán's room. The aroma of the stew made his room feel warm and inviting in spite of the Louisiana heat outside. Once in the room, they looked at each other.

Rónán cleared his throat. "Um," he felt bashful. "I'm going to need the shirt. If you want it fixed, that is."

Abel looked confused for a moment and then laughed and began unbuttoning the shirt from the collar and working his hands down toward his waist.

"I already told you, I'm not the brightest," Abel said.

He slipped the shirt from his body, revealing the lean muscle that Rónán had admired at the watering hole, Rónán hoped the dusk creeping in the window left the room dim enough so that Abel would not notice his flushed face. He turned his head to be safe.

Abel handed the shirt to Rónán. It was still slightly damp with sweat from working in the sun.

"Sorry about that," Abel said. For the first time, Rónán thought Abel looked embarrassed. There was something bashful in the way he scratched the back of his neck as he apologized for the sweat slicked to his shirt.

"Don't be. Make yourself comfortable."

Rónán sat on the stool in front of his mother's vanity. Living alone for the last decade, he hadn't felt the need to accumulate any additional seating, so he gestured for Abel to sit on his bed.

Now shirtless, Abel sprawled himself on the lumpy mattress, half lying down, half sitting, his back against the wall. Rónán wondered if Abel was reading his mind and purposefully lying in a way that showed off his body.

Abel shifted his weight to find a comfortable position. Then, reaching behind him, Abel pulled out the patchwork seal that Rónán kept in his bed.

"And who is this?" he asked.

Not wanting to meet his gaze, Rónán busied himself threading the eye of the needle, his nervous tremor making that difficult.

"My ma made it," he replied shyly.

Abel turned the stuffed animal over in his hands, running his hands along the stitches and feeling the textures of the fabrics.

"You must really like seals," Abel observed.

Rónán pushed the needle through the shoulder of Abel's shirt, weighing his response. "When I was a boy. My ma called me *little seal*," Rónán shared. "So, she made that for me."

"*Little seal*?" Abel looked at Rónán quizzically.

"Yes, little seal."

They sat in silence, the only sounds the light scratching of Rónán's sewing and the quiet bubbling from the pot on the cookstove. Abel looked expectant, waiting for Ronan to continue. Rónán could feel his eyes on him, and the unanswered question that still lingered in the air.

"When Ma was a girl, her ma told her a story of a little seal. And I guess she liked it so much, that's what she called me," Rónán explained.

"Well, what's the story?"

"Just an old children's story."

"Well, I was *a children* once," Abel laughed.

This time, Rónán did meet his gaze. He could see genuine interest reflected in Abel's face. Not patronizing, simply curious.

Looking down at his line of stitches, Rónán began. "A long time ago, on the shores of Ireland, there was a seal. She was a curious creature, and almost every day, she would swim too close to shore. The other seals always told her to be careful, not to approach the land, but she didn't listen.

"One day, when she was playing too close to shore, a big wave kicked up and carried her all the way to dry land. When the seal woke up and realized she was no longer in the sea, she found that she had transformed into a woman, a human woman. As a human, she explored dry land, eventually finding and falling in love with a fisherman who lived alone in a cabin by the sea. She married the fisherman and had children with him. She called her children *rónáns*. It means *little seals*.”

Abel listened intently, hugging the stuffed seal to his chest. His mouth hung slightly open as if he were waiting to ask a question.

Rónán considered him for a moment but continued speaking while pulling the thread through Abel’s shirt. “After years of living with her family, the woman still longed for the sea and for the other seals. Eventually, she came across a gray mass that she realized was her seal skin hidden by the fisherman. She put her seal skin back on and returned to the sea.”

“She left her family?” Abel asked, leaning into the story.

“Not quite,” Rónán continued. “She became the first selkie.”

Seeing the question on Abel’s face, Rónán explained, “a creature that lives near the waters of Ireland. Anyway, the selkie missed her family. From that day on, she could choose her form at will, magicking between a human woman and a seal. She could stay close to shore and watch over her husband and family.”

“And where is she now?” Abel asked.

Rónán was confused, “What do you mean?”

“The mother—where is she now?”

Rónán pulled the last few stitches, knitting together the two sides of the ripped cotton fabric. “It’s just a story,” he said without looking up. “They tell it to kids.”

“Well, I think it’s a good story, *little seal*,” Abel said with a twinkle in his eye. He held the stuffed animal more carefully now, as if it were precious and easily breakable.

“Here.” Rónán held out the shirt. “Try it on.”

There was a small, closet sized changing room on the first floor of the shop, but Abel stood up and faced away from Rónán.

“Help me out?” He asked.

Rónán rose from the wooden stool and held the shirt as Abel fed his arms through each sleeve. Rónán watched Abel’s muscles cascade in movement. Standing here behind him, Rónán realized just how broad Abel's shoulders were from his work at the docks. Rónán eyes lingered on the dark red, crusted scratch across Abel's right shoulder.

"I can give you something for that." Rónán's voice almost quavered. "My ma used to make medicines and things. I have a bottle somewhere…" his voice trailed off.

"Something for what?" Abel asked.

A fire started in the pit of Rónán's stomach. "That cut on your back. Let me help you. Give me a moment." Rónán stood and bounded down the steps, two at a time. Rifling among the vials under the counter, he pulled back a clear glass bottle with a pale green liquid inside. He uncorked the top and sniffed, finding the aroma he was looking for—rosemary and mint. He tucked the bottle into a spare piece of cloth and made his way back up to Abel.

As he entered the room, Rónán took in the sight of Abel. Abel turned his head, peering over his shoulder and grinning. Rónán's pulse quickened. Crossing the room, Rónán dabbed a few clear drops of the green liquid onto the cloth. Delicately, he wiped away the dried blood on Abel's shoulder. Through the cloth, he could feel the warmth radiating from Abel's skin.

"Done," he said, as he helped Abel lift the cotton shirt onto his shoulder.

Abel tugged at the shirt as he turned around for Rónán to examine his work. Bringing his arms out wide exposed his golden, tanned abdomen.

"How do I look?" Abel asked with a grin, "Handsome as ever, I'm sure."

Somewhere in his chest, the hummingbird took flight again, no doubt trying to escape the flames consuming Rónán from the inside.

The heat rising to his face, he whispered, "Perfect."

Something hung in the air between them as they looked at each other, Abel grinning and Rónán not quite sure where to place his eyes. If Abel could sense the fog created from the heat dissipating off Rónán, he did not let on. But it was there, and Rónán was sure if he reached his hand out, he would even feel the vapor lick at his fingers. His mind seemed empty. The only thing he was aware of was Abel.

"Oh, no way!" Abel suddenly said, calling Rónán's attention back to the room, "Do you play?" He gestured to a black leather case that leaned atop an old wooden box. The case had sat there so long, Rónán had nearly forgotten about it. Inside was the fiddle Aislyn had brought from Ireland. Because Rónán never learned to play, the case had not been opened or the strings plucked for the last decade.

Rónán shook his head no.

"When I was a boy, my momma made me—and Douglas, too—learn from Clementine's mom. May I?" Abel asked, gesturing toward the case.

Rónán nodded his head, watching his friend reach for the case. Abel sat on the edge of the bed and gently brought the case to his lap, as if it was a baby to bounce on his knee. Abel rolled his sleeves up to his elbows, more carefully than he had done in the bayou. Opening the lid, he reverently lifted the instrument from its sleep and began plucking the strings.

"I haven't played in years," he said, turning the pegs at the neck of the instrument, stretching the strings into harmony. "After Momma and Daddy died, Douglas made me stop my lessons. He never really liked it—thought it was a waste of time."

Abel examined the instrument, running his fingers along the inlaid filigree on the fiddle's neck. "Douglas made me get a job at the docks, and after my first day of work, I never saw my fiddle again. I never did find out what he did with it. Probably chucked it in the fireplace."

Abel seemed pleased with the notes the plucked strings produced. He reached back into the case for the bow. He tightened the horse hairs and slid a block of a sap-like substance across them, creating a small puff of white dust in the air. He returned to his half-reclining position on the bed, shouldered the violin under his chin, and pulled the bow across the strings. In a woody warm voice, the violin sang. The sound reminded Rónán of the feeling of running his hands through warm, dry sand. Abel played a familiar tune, somewhere between a playful ballad and a funeral dirge. Rónán could not quite place it, but echoes of a miner's daughter drowning in a river rippled in his mind.

Rónán sat back on the stool as his friend played. Abel closed his eyes, seemingly lost in the music. His fingers knowingly danced across the ebony neck of the fiddle. Rónán couldn't help but be impressed. His friend with the hard body and strong hands now seemed so delicate. He found himself captivated by the roiling movement in Abel's forearms, muscle rising and falling in time with the music. The hummingbird beat against Ronan's chest trying to push through his skin.

Abel drew the final note of the song from the hollow depths of the violin with a slow, exaggerated vibrato. He opened his eyes and winked. "I'm a little rusty."

Rónán sat in the vacuum created when the music ended. Images of Abel raced through his mind as his heartbeat quickened in his ears. Abel extracted from the violin case a piece of yellowing paper.

"What is this?" Abel asked, handing the dry, cracking paper to Rónán.

Immediately, Rónán recognized it. On the page he saw carefully scrawled music and recognized the familiar tilt of his mother's writing. Worn by the years, the edges of the notes Aislyn drew on the page had blurred to a softness created by the slowly bleeding ink.

"It was my ma's—a song from her homeland," Rónán said, without consciously realizing how he knew. "Can you play it?"

Abel took the sheet back from Rónán and considered it for a moment. He brought the fiddle back to his chin and began to play. Immediately, Rónán was pulled through time. The old melody filled the shop as his mother took a break from her sewing work. She began to sing as she played, her voice crystal clear above the reedy sounds of the strings. Rónán watched his mother with admiration, only it wasn't his mother.

With tears in his eyes, Rónán listened while Abel played. This was more than just a tune. IIt was a blessing. He felt the warmth of his tears on his face, and it made his affection for his friend more intense. He continued watching and listening as Abel played. This didn't feel like a performance; it felt like a conversation happening in the silence between them. As Abel reached the end of the page, he looked up and saw Rónán's tears. He suddenly stopped playing, leaving the final phrase unfinished.

"Are you okay?" Abel asked.

Sniffing and wiping his eyes with the backs of his hands, Rónán nodded, but his feelings overwhelmed him. His tears became a flood, and before he knew it, he was sobbing into his hands.

"Hey," Abel laid the violin in its case, reached out to Ronan, and placed his hands on Rónán's knees. His palms radiated warmth where they touched Rónán.

"Look—I'm sorry," Abel said with a slight stutter.

"No," Rónán sniffed, "No, it's okay. It's just—"

But he didn't know what it *just* was. The tears continued. Then, he felt himself being pulled to his feet. Without another word, Abel wrapped his arms around Rónán. And, for the first time in over a decade, Rónán allowed himself to be held.

Rónán wasn't sure how long they remained this way. His soft sobs and the quiet boiling on the cookstove were the only sounds in the room. After what felt like both an eternity and an instant, Rónán pulled back. His green eyes met Abel's. The two looked at each other, not speaking, arms around each other. Through his tears, Rónán saw Abel's face with his soft, pink lips, and felt the hummingbird flutter. The room stood still, seemingly growing warmer.

Rónán felt himself moving closer to Abel. Was Abel also moving closer to him? All Rónán could hear was the thrumming beat in his ears; all he could see was the glowing face of Abel.

Suddenly, a loud pop from the fire crackling in the cookstove shook them both to attention. Blinking and dropping his arms from the embrace, Rónán backed away from Abel.

"I'm sorry," he said. "It's just been so long since I've heard Ma's music."

Abel cleared his throat, struggling to find his words. "No," he said hoarsely. "I'm sorry I upset you. I better get goin'. Douglas won't be happy if I'm out so late again."

Rónán nodded.

"Thanks for my shirt," Abel said with a shy smile as he fastened each of the buttons hurriedly. "I really appreciate your help, tailor."

Something about the way Abel said *tailor* made Rónán sense some kind of door closing. Without another word, Abel pushed past him onto the landing. Rónán listened as his footfalls retreated down the stairs and out the door.

Rónán let out a shaky sigh. He extinguished the flames in the cookstove and peered into the pot containing his supper. As he watched the bubbles in the pot slow to a stillness, Rónán kept picturing Abel's face looking back at him. The desire he felt there in the room was obvious now. He wanted nothing more than to kiss Abel, to bring his lips to Abel's while they continued to hold one another. This realization sent shame creeping up Rónán's spine. Once again, he found himself confused.

After letting his stew cool, Rónán ladled the thick, brown stuff into a bowl. He ate in silence, missing the music that had reverberated off the walls. When he finished the last spoonful, Rónán walked downstairs to his shop. After closing the curtains and locking his door, he decided to return to bed. He would continue working in the morning.

As he laid in bed, Rónán kept replaying the moments he shared with Abel in his room, picturing Abel's arms, the muscles in his back, the golden flecks in his eyes, and the pink softness of his lips. But Rónán thought that he couldn't keep thinking this way. He did not want to jeopardize the one friendship he had made in Bridewater. He wanted things to go back to normal. *He wanted nothing more than for himself to be normal.*

With a sigh, Rónán rolled over in bed, his back to the wall. As he closed his eyes, Rónán felt the room fade to blackness. Eventually he slept.

* * *

A faint, choking noise woke Rónán with a start. He opened his eyes, blinking quickly, trying to adjust his vision in the dark room. He rolled over to check for signs of morning through the window next to his bed, but only darkness waited beyond the glass. A sickly feeling burned in his throat. He felt like eyes watched him from the darkness, just beyond his own field of vision.

Rónán opened his eyes wide and looked across the room, trying not to make any movement. His room seemed even darker than before, but he caught one brief flicker of movement. He stared into the corner opposite his bed, just beyond the vanity, but it seemed impossibly black. As his ears adjusted to the stillness of the night, he heard the familiar murmuring that had been haunting him.

Rónán fumbled for a match from the box atop his vanity, almost scared to reach across the abyss that was the space between his bed and where the box lay. Hands shaking, it was all he could muster to strike the match in a single, swift movement. As he lit the oil lamp, a burst of light temporarily filled the room. In the flickering darkness, he could see her knobby, swollen joints, her sunken, bruised face, her slack jaw, and her stitched up eyes and mouth.

Her urgent whispers sent a cold shiver up his spine, as if someone dragged their fingernails along the length of his back. Rónán stared at the woman, and though her eyes were sewn shut, he had the distinct feeling that she was staring right back at him. The bride's gown, seeping and dripping with salty water, swelled in waves of fabric as she clumsily shifted her feet, staggering toward Rónán's bed.

He was shaking, crying. Like a child again, he threw himself under his blankets, wishing and praying—no, pleading—for the woman to leave.

The drag of her footsteps grew closer and closer. The sound of wet, rotting flesh thumping against the wooden floor made Rónán's stomach turn, and hot, sour bile flooded the back of his throat.

The bride approached his bed. From the uneven flicker of light thrown by his lamp, Rónán could see her silhouette, stretched to a more grotesque, elongated version of herself. The gray shadows of her hands slowly reached up. Peeking over the protection of the blanket, Rónán could see that they were clasped together at an odd, almost broken angle. Her long, slender fingers wriggled closer to him, like spiders crawling along his quilt.

His breath quickened as he fought to draw in enough air, suddenly feeling lightheaded.

Her fingers stretched closer.

Rónán's heartbeat throbbed in his temples.

The shadow of her frame bent over, leaning ever closer to Rónán. Her whispering grew louder, more desperate. Rónán clapped his hands over his ears, but he couldn't take his eyes away from the phantom before him. Any second now, her snakelike fingers would wriggle under the blanket and heave it back, ripping away Rónán's only protection. She was close enough that he could smell her rotten stench, like a puddle of stagnant sea water. It was all too much. The bile at the back of his throat, he screamed.

"IT'S NOT ME!" He repeated, "IT'S NOT ME! I'M NOT HIM!"

Maybe it was in his head, or maybe it actually happened, but he seemed to sense the bride stop moving.

"I'M NOT YOUR HUSBAND! IT'S NOT ME! IT'S NOT ME! IT'S NOT ME!" Rónán screamed from under his blanket. He was heaving with guttural, throaty, breathless sobs. He kicked his feet wildly, trying anything that might keep the woman from advancing closer.

Shaking, he opened his eyes. The shadow was gone. With a desperate exhalation, Rónán threw his blankets free and scanned each corner of the room, wrenching his eyes from corner to corner. He grabbed the oil lamp and waved it around the room, illuminating every cranny the light would reach.

She was gone. The only sign that she had been there, the only thing that told Rónán he wasn't going crazy was, like yesterday, the set of wet footprints that started at the corner of his room and stopped at the edge of his bed.

He rose. Desperately scrounging around in both his room and his shop, he gathered every candle and lamp he could find. He lit them hurriedly, using almost every match he had left, and burning the tips of his fingers in the process. He spaced the lights around his room, creating a faint, orange light. There was something oddly sacramental about the rows of candles and lamps, only Rónán wasn't making an offering; he was constructing a prayer in desperation. When his room was finally lit, Rónán cradled himself in bed and waited for morning.

Chapter 6

When the candlelight no longer fought the darkness, Rónán warily removed himself from his bed. His knees ached in protest after being bent against his chest for the last few hours. He carefully extinguished each flame, returning each candle and lamp to its proper place in his shop.

Rónán peeled back the curtains on his front window slowly, hoping that nothing or no one waited for him on the other side. When all he saw was a view of the empty docks, he relaxed his shoulders and rubbed the bridge of his nose between his thumb and forefinger. The pressure in his skull made him feel as if he were underwater. Reaching into the small bag below the countertop, Rónán retrieved a red-and-white striped peppermint, removing the wrapper and popping it into his mouth. He exhaled forcefully, intentionally, hoping the shock of the cool mint would give him the energy he needed to work through the day.

His eyes traveled to the window again. The sky hanging above the bay was overcast, illuminated in splotchy gray. The sun cast strangely undulating shadows across the road. They reminded Rónán of the bride coming closer to him. For a sickly moment, a bitter pain gnawed at his stomach. He thought he saw her fingers reaching out from the arching shadows of the trees.

Closer. Closer.

"No," Rónán shook his head. His hands convulsed, as if they were struggling to grip onto reality. "Please, no."

Rónán inhaled, pulling a sleeve across the wet that fear left on his face.

The familiar faces of the men of Bridewater began filing past his windows. Rónán found himself watching them, checking for Abel, knowing the young man's glow would stand out amidst the gloom of the day. But when Rónán saw the familiar yellowing cotton shirt and olive trousers, he found himself shrinking. He pressed his back against the wall, making himself small, hidden out of view of his windows.

What am I doing? Rónán thought.

Crouching against the wall, he could barely see Abel. His mind replayed images from the night before. Abel, half-dressed, lounging on his bed. The rippling muscles of Abel's back as he put on the patched shirt. Abel's forearms, so delicate but so strong, as they pulled music out of his mother's fiddle. Abel's face, his lips, so soft and inviting. But the images of Abel faded and rematerialized as *her*. The bride's wet, slapping feet creaked up his stairs. Creeping along the floorboards in her convulsive, stammering walk, and she flung Rónán's door open, her hands grasping for something through the emptiness. The realization came to Rónán like a match struck in the dark.

Each time the bride came to call was directly after Rónán had seen Abel. Rónán could not help but think that perhaps the bride was tied to Abel, looking for him and not Rónán. Or maybe, she saw what was floating in the back of Rónán's mind. Like a shark circling its prey, the bride came to consume Rónán for the embarrassing, perverted, corrupted thoughts he held about Abel. She saw Rónán's sin, and she wanted to rip it out of him.

A wash of resolve stained with sadness overtook him. He knew that he should not keep seeing Abel. He knew he should erase these feelings for Abel and think of him only as a friend to keep company with. If only he could actually do this! He would be alone, like he had been for ten years. The dull bruise of loneliness would return but, he hoped beyond hope, perhaps the bride would not.

As if he had sensed Rónán there surreptitiously watching, Abel craned his head to look at the tailor shop and scanned the window. Rónán held his breath, pressing himself into the wall. When Abel turned back toward the docks and away from the shop, Rónán closed the curtains and shut out the world beyond the shop.

Rónán shook his hands out, flexing and clenching them in turn. He was fighting to control the tremor, so he did what worked best, he got to work. He wanted to finish Helene's gown.

He considered his sketches for a moment, choosing one that was smart enough to look nice, but casual enough that he could make it quickly and well. Exasperated, he brought his palm to his forehead. Helene was a petite girl, favoring her mother's slender, build, but Rónán did not know her measurements. He would need to get them before sewing the dress, even before creating a pattern. He had already planned to return the preacher's clothes today, so he would make a stop at the general store during his errands. This would ruin the surprise, he knew, but it was better to ruin the surprise than to ruin the garment.

Rónán found the folded pile of the preacher's clothes and placed them into the bag they were dropped off in. With a pair of black-handled, metal scissors, he cut a small swatch of the dyed cloth to bring with him. He figured if he had to ruin the surprise, he might as well build anticipation by showing Helene the beautiful color of the fabric. He tore a single piece of paper from the same notebook he had sketched in and rolled a small pencil into it. Thinking again, he tore one of the sketches out of the book, wrapping it around the already bundled paper and pencil and shoved them into his pocket with the scrap of purple fabric. Cradling the bag of clothes in his arms, Rónán walked toward the front door but, before grasping the doorknob, paused and decided to avoid walking directly past the docks in order to avoid Abel and the thoughts he was determined to banish. He turned and exited the shop instead through the green painted door at the back. He stepped into the alleyway. The morning was overcast, with occasional, distant rumbles of thunder reverberating through Bridewater. Though the gray sky threatened rain, the ground was still dry. Rónán saw the orange tabby cat slinking in the shadows. It darted its eyes towards him and froze. When the cat decided he was not a threat, it continued ambling through the tall weeds lining the backs of the buildings. Rónán took an immediate right and crossed the road toward the chapel.

As he approached the Baptist hall, Rónán glanced towards the graveyard. The rows of mossy stones stood like a strange, short forest. He found himself wondering how far back the dates would go if he wandered through. When the flu spread through town, an outcrop of new headstones had been added, but others were so old that the etching on them was barely legible, weathered by years of ocean breeze and swamp water. Rónán pondered whether he and his mother would have been buried there following their own deaths, but a part of him knew they would always be kept separate from the rest of the population of Bridewater. Sadly, Rónán would never have to confront this question for his mother.

He padded up to the front steps leading to the chapel. He left the bag of clothes on the porch in front of the large double doors and rapped quietly on the knotted wood of the door to signal that he'd dropped the delivery off. Then he retreated from the church before anyone could answer the door. As he glanced back, he thought he saw the curtain part just enough for someone to peer out the small window to the left of the front door, signaling he had completed another successful transaction.

Compelled by some unseen force, Rónán's gaze briefly flashed toward the docks that were only yards away. Out of the corner of his eye, he saw something that made his stomach drop. Abel stooped, placing a crate on the ground at the entrance to the docks where someone would lift it into the next transport. As if connected by an invisible string, Abel looked up in time to see Rónán. With a grin, he placed one hand on his belt line and waved with the other.. Rónán looked away and quickened his pace, ignoring Abel. Instead of walking back through the grassy alley, Rónán passed to the front side of the second row of shops.

Rónán began making his way toward the general store. The line of shops on this side of Bridewater seemed to be less ravaged by the salty sea air than the shops facing the bay. Though they were aging, they were not in the same state of disrepair as his own storefront and the butchery. The most decayed building was the old post office that had remained unused and uncared for all of Rónán's memory. It seemed a metaphor for Bridewater, past its prime and ignored. It had potential to be something more than an empty husk, but it was not capitalized on.

Walking along this side of town, Rónán was surprised to find that he didn't have the same familiar feeling of being watched. Yes, lines of homes and the fronts of these shops faced him, but he did not feel the prick of eyes moving on him as he walked. When he arrived at the general store, Rónán pushed the door open, sounding the chime again. Henriette, rounding the corner from the back offices at the sound of the bell, greeted him.

"Hello, Rónán. Is there something I can help you with?" She charmed in her southern style.

"Good morning," Rónán began bashfully. "It's about Helene's dress."

"Oh?" Henriette exclaimed. "What is it? Is something wrong? Will it not be done in time?"

"Oh no, nothing like that," Rónán said. "It's just, I don't have her measurements. I know it was meant to be a surprise, but I want it to be as perfect as possible."

Henriette chuckled, "Oh, I should have known. One moment," she held up one hand and leaned her head back toward the empty space behind her. "Helene, please come here for a moment."

Helene's muffled voice returned, "Yes, *maman*!" And the sound of her footfalls reached the room where Rónán awaited.

"*Mon ange*," Mrs. Hebert said, nodding toward the tailor. "Rónán here has agreed to make a gown, a gift from your father and me, for you to take with you to seminary."

At this, Helene beamed and clapped her hands. "Oh, *maman*! Thank you!"

As she hugged her daughter and patted her back, Henriette continued, "He is going to need to take your measurements; take him with you to *papa's* office."

Helene practically skipped over to Rónán and grasped both of his hands in hers, "Follow me," she said with a squeal. Rónán struggled to keep up as Helene practically dragged him to the back office.

They entered a small, dark room at the back of the general store. A heavy desk sat in the center of the room with a padded chair behind. On the wall facing the door, there was a stone fireplace with lines of photos of the Hebert family framed above it, and a small window. Helene bounded across the room to open the curtains, flooding the room with light. She turned, her bright smile gleaming at Rónán.

"Now what?" she asked, excitement still flooding her eyes.

Rónán quickly explained to her the measurements he would need to take. He wrapped the measuring tape around her waist, arms, shoulders, and bust in turn, asking for her permission each time. He also measured various lengths of her body. As he did, Rónán recorded each on the paper he brought.

"All done," Rónán said after a few minutes of measuring. He smiled at her shyly, "Would you like to see my idea for the dress?"

Helene could not look more excited if she tried. Her dark eyes lit up, reflecting the sunlight streaming into the room, and her rosy cheeks grew even brighter.

"Oh, please!" she exclaimed.

Rónán fished the sketch out of his pocket. "This is the shape I was considering. And this," he fished the fabric swatch out of his pocket, "is the color."

Helene gasped. She accepted the drawing and the swatch of mauve fabric delicately, as if she were cradling a baby. She closed her eyes, savoring the moment.

"*C'est belle,*" she said. Rónán observed a twinkle in her eyes. She smiled, "Maybe now I can get Abel to notice me."

In a blink, Rónán fixed his posture, forcing himself to become still. "Abel?" he asked.

Helene pursed her lips together, stifling a smile and looking toward the floor. "Oh, he's just so cute."

Rónán felt a flush rising in his cheeks, and he tried to shake it away with a quick jerk of his head.

"I've always fancied him," Helene chimed. "He used to always tease me at church—pull my hair and all that."

Rónán cleared his throat, trying to swallow the sour taste in the back of his throat, "Oh, I didn't... I didn't know you two were close." He busied himself with the tape measure still in his hands.

Helene laughed, "Close? I wouldn't say that we are close. I never see him at the chapel anymore. Besides, *maman* says that I need to focus on school. There's always time for boys later." She rolled her eyes.

Rónán continued fidgeting with the tools in his hands, unsure of what to do or say next.

Helene picked up the soft square of mauve fabric and ran it between her fingers. "You know, this reminds me of something your mama made me when I was a child."

Rónán blinked in surprise.

"Hold on," she said, and she retreated out of the room.

Rónán stood alone in the room, watching the particles of dust float in the rays of sun coming in the windows. After a moment, Helene returned, with a white cloth folded over her arms. She carried it carefully, reverently, as if the small fabric could shatter with the wrong touch.

"Here," she said, handing the cloth to Rónán.

Rónán accepted it and recognized it right away. He had laundered the blanket for the Hebert's many times before, even recently. The white cloth was embroidered with light violet blooms. Rónán had never considered before that it was made by his mother, but upon looking closely, he recognized her signature stitches. While they were neat, they seemed to be an interesting mix of parallel, diagonal, and cross-hatched lines. Holding the cloth now made Rónán feel a twinge of sadness. Had they been apart for so long that he couldn't recognize her work anymore?

Unsure if Helene recognized his sadness or if she just wanted to continue speaking, Rónán listened to her recount her story. "You know, when I was a child, I got sick with that nasty flu," she began quietly. Rónán knew this. She was one of the only people in Bridewater to catch the flu and live to tell.

"*Maman* and *papa* said I nearly died. They watched my face turn purple when I couldn't breathe and felt the heat burning beneath my skin. They tried everything to make me feel better, but nothing worked. That is, until your mama visited."

An image played in the recess of Rónán's mind of his mother walking out the door with small vials of her homemade tinctures.

"Your mama came to me. She gave my parents some medicine and brought me this blanket. *Maman* said it was like Aislyn was an angel. That same night, I opened my eyes and started to breathe again. I've slept with this blanket every night since."

Rónán fingered the delicately stitched flowers.

Helene grasped his hands in her own and looked up at him. "Rónán, I think you have your mama's gift. I…*We* are so thankful."

Rónán cleared his throat and made a stuttering exhalation. "I have to go," he choked. "Please, tell your mother bye. I'll bring the dress by the store when it's done."

Without waiting for a reply, Rónán dropped Helene's hands and headed out of the office and into the main general store. Henriette stood there. Noticing Rónán's puffy, reddening eyes, she gave him a startled look, but before she could say anything, Rónán strode out the door.

Moving quickly, Rónán almost ran to the stone walkway between buildings. The hollow pain in his stomach made him double over. He placed his hands on his knees until it passed. The wound of losing his mother, and now not even being able to recognize her work was too much.

An orange blur swam into his vision. The ginger tomcat mewed up at him, stretching its legs out and thrusting its rear end toward the sky. The sudden interruption made Rónán laugh. He patted the cat and it flopped to its side and began biting and scratching at his hand.

Rónán wiped his nose with his free hand. "Hey! Don't bite me, you mangey thing." He laughed, half shooing the cat away.

Rónán followed the animal into the alley and watched it duck under one of the neighboring buildings. Not wanting to be seen, he hurried to the backdoor of his shop, passing a line of laundry hanging on the clothesline. The sky overhead was still overcast, and distant rumbles sounded over the bay.

Rónán entered the back door and locked it behind him. He felt a small tremor in his hands as thoughts of his mother bubbled to the surface of his mind again. With the new measurements, and the blessings of Henriette and Helene, Rónán decided to do the thing he knew would take his mind away from his sadness. He got to work.

Chapter 7

When Rónán's eyes strained to see in the muted light of the shop, he realized how late the day had become. He spent most of his afternoon drafting and redrafting patterns for Helene's dress. When he was finally happy with the pieces and they matched the measurements he had taken earlier in the day, Rónán began to assemble the dress. He started by cutting into the fabric. Before making the first cut, he always felt a momentary dread. That was the point of no return, but as soon as the shears bit their way through the fabric with a satisfying *shink*, his anxiety dissipated. He painstakingly pinned the remaining sheets of paper to the yards of mauve fabric, tracing dusty white lines with chalk to mark where he would cut. Rónán knew that some might find this sequence tedious, but he loved every part of this creative process. He repeatedly blinked as he tried to correct the blur that crept into his vision in the dimly lit room. It was time for him to stop for the evening. He neatly layered the pieces on the flat surface of his workspace and yawned.

Rónán felt a tight knot in the space between his shoulder blades. He clasped his hands together and reached toward the ceiling, stretching from one side to the other. His arms dropped to his sides, and he began to roll his head in a circular motion around his neck. He bent backwards, creating a slight arch with his spine. As he stretched, light cracks and pops sounded as the tension escaped from his muscles. He then cracked his knuckles enjoying the percussive sound. Closing his eyes, Rónán took a long, sighing breath in through his nose. He held it for a moment, then released it in a wide yawn.

Rónán opened his eyes. Though he was tired, and he ached from his work, he felt a buzzing energy, something close to the feeling of joy. He couldn't remember the last time he got to create a piece of clothing, not just fix a lady's hem or patch a man's pants. He was thankful for the distraction, suddenly realizing that he had not thought about the bride or Abel for hours.

With the lamp in his hand sending flickering shadows across his walls, Rónán walked up the stairs to his bedroom. He was exhausted. His lack of sleep hung over him like a heavy, wet blanket. He changed into his sleepwear, some loose fitting, white woolen garments, and climbed into bed. Rónán still felt that light, electric buzz from working on Helene's gown, but as soon as his head hit the pillow, he was breathing steadily, deeply asleep.

*   *   *

A soft, gray light dispersed through the embroidered curtains over his bedroom window. Rónán slowly opened his eyes. The muted, concussive sounds of men working at the docks alerted him that he had slept longer than he intended, but it was the first time he had slept through the night since before the bride made her first appearance. With that, he realized the bride had not visited him the previous night. His heart felt lighter. His thoughts had not lingered on Abel and the bride chose not to visit. He felt as if the plague that had followed him no longer haunted him.

Rónán rocked himself to a seated position on the edge of his bed. His joints ached, numb and burning. He stretched his fingers, clenching and releasing them, feeling the searing tenderness with each movement.

Of course, he thought. He finally had work that excited him, and he woke up sick. He moved down the stairs and into his shop. The beginnings of Helene's dress greeted him. He crossed to the counter, grabbing a peppermint and tossed it into his mouth. The cool mint soothed the soreness in his throat, but he knew he would need more. Rónán scratched in his brain for one of his mother's herbal remedies. Finding none, he retrieved her journal that detailed various plants and their uses. He found an entry for something his mother called purple coneflower. In her hand, she wrote that, "when prepared correctly" it could help with "joint pain, toothaches, and sickness." His mother's tidy script explained how to use every part of the plant, from oil distilled from its roots to tea brewed from its petals and leaves. He made a mental note of the places where it grew and trotted back up the stairs to prepare it.

In a corner of his room, he found the same set of clothes he wore when he last went into the bayou. Though they were still lightly damp with sweat, he pulled them on and the muddy boots he also never got around to cleaning, Rónán examined himself in the mirror. The purple bags under his eyes were less pronounced, and the whites of his eyes finally showed more white than red. He started to pull his hair back into a knot when he heard a knocking on his front door.

"Rónán?" Abel's familiar voice called.

Three more loud raps sounded against the door.

"Rónán, it's Abel. Are you in there?"

Rónán's eyes widened. For the first time in days, he had had a dreamless, visitor-less sleep. Something in the back of his mind told him that seeing Abel, speaking to him, would change that for the worse. Rónán held his breath, daring not to move.

There was one more fast set of knocks. "I just wanna talk, Rónán. If you're in there, if you can hear me, come by later." With that, Abel left, his footsteps retreating from the boardwalk in front of the tailor shop.

Rónán waited a moment, still not wanting to stir. When he finally felt he had waited long enough, he parted his bedroom curtains the smallest sliver and sneaked a peak. He could see Abel's back as he walked back toward the docks. There seemed to be a heaviness in the way he walked away, his shoulders slumped. They didn't carry their usual weightlessness.

Rónán closed the curtains. He felt a sadness but willed it away. He finished pulling his hair back and walked back down to the shop. He thought about what he should bring along on his search for coneflowers, but he decided his pockets would suffice. Trying to avoid the workers at the dock—well, one worker in particular—Rónán made his way to the flowered door at the back of his shop and stepped out into the gloomy day. Like the previous day, the sky was gray and cloudy, but it had yet to release its rain. While the low cloud cover kept the sun from making the day unbearable, it was still Louisiana in June, and the day was warm and muggy.

According to his mother's notes, purple coneflower was easier to find than some of the other plants she detailed. She wrote that it preferred sunlight and tended to grow in dryer spots. There weren't a lot of dry places near Bridewater, but his mother's notes chronicled a hilly spot between Bridewater Bay and the bayou where the plant could be found growing on a raised, dry patch of earth.

Rónán followed her described path—this time, walking toward the abandoned post office. As he approached the small, wooden building, Rónán noted its ornamental federal regality, but even that hadn't protected it from being boarded up. He always wondered why the postmaster was never replaced. Probably it had something to do with the way Bridewater didn't seem to grow, shrinking instead due to the encroaching wetlands and its disappearing population.

For about a mile, Rónán followed the road that led out of Bridewater, winding through trees and overgrown grass. When he came to a row of wild, prickly-leaved holly, he turned toward the north. There beyond the holly was a lightly trodden path, where years of footfalls had ever so slightly halted the growth of plant life. If he wasn't looking for the path, he was sure he would have overlooked it. As he walked along the path through thickets of tall, scratchy grasses, he wondered if his mother had worked this path into the ground. For a moment, he felt connected with her again.

A few times while following the path, he had to backtrack to be sure he was going in the right direction. He continued on for what felt like hours in the humid heat, sweat suctioning his shirt to his back. When he came across a quartet of rocks that were oddly, unnaturally stacked, he knew he had reached the right place. In the yellowing dry grass around him, he saw tall, skinny purple flowers. They looked exactly like his mother's drawings. He carefully dug into the earth, removing the flowers at their roots. He took just enough for what he wanted to brew and one extra to propagate in his back garden. With the flowers bunched in his hand, he sat on one of the rocks his mother had described. Reaching behind him, he pulled a long piece of golden grass from the earth and wove the grass around the stems of the flowers to bind them together.

Out of the corner of his eye, Rónán saw a flash of movement. He looked to his right and saw a butterfly swimming through the air erratically. Its thin wings of iridescent blue faded into black at the edges and were speckled with dots of white and brilliant, tangerine orange. The butterfly fluttered closer to Rónán. As he held his breath, it landed on his forearm, right over the scar where his mother had sewn him up. He didn't want to move and scare it but could not help smiling as he watched it open and close its papery wings on the length of his arm, showing off its beautiful colors. He tried recalling a story his mother told him about butterflies, but he couldn't remember the details. He thought this location might be important to the story. After a moment, the butterfly fluttered its wings again and took to the air. It floated around his face for a moment before the breeze carried it away from him.

Rónán gripped the bundle of flowers and started retracing his steps back to Bridewater. The path, more familiar now, was easier to traverse on his way back. As he walked, thunder sounded above him. The sky was still heavy with gray, but the rain didn't come.

As the rows of buildings in Bridewater Bay came into view, Rónán suddenly felt anxious. He wanted to avoid any path that took him near the butchery, near Abel, so he took a detour that would bring him back through the graveyard past the church to the mouth of the alley behind his shop. As he weaved between the gravestones, he saw something that alarmed him. Standing on the front steps of the chapel were Douglas and Clementine. They were looking up at and talking to Clementine's parents, the preacher and his wife, who stood on the narrow porch outside the church doors.

The preacher and his wife were both short, round people. The man was balding, with tufts of gray hair on his temples that resembled wafts of cigarette smoke. His wife had salt and pepper hair pulled back into a tight knot on the back of her head. Clementine seemed so different from her parents. While they were round and red-faced, she was almost sunken, Both the preacher and his wife were dressed nicely. Even from a distance, Rónán could see the shirt buttons over the preacher's gut threatening to give way.He made a mental note to reinforce them the next time he did their laundering.

Rónán felt all four sets of eyes find him. He guessed he was an unusual sight amongst the mossy stones of the departed. He gave a polite nod and waved to them. The preacher and his wife seemed content not to speak, so he fixed his gaze forward toward the alley across the road. He could see the orange cat stalking something. He focused all of his attention on the cat, willing the people near him to ignore him so he could continue walking. Behind him, he heard Douglas' low, growling voice cut across the lawn.

"Give me a minute," the butcher said to the others. His heavy feet kicked through the grass after Rónán. "Boy," he said.

Rónán stopped. Feeling nervous, he turned to face the large man. Douglas' dark, greasy hair was combed to the side. He crossed his thick arms in front of his chest and spoke again.

"Abel's been lookin' for you," he growled in his slow southern accent. "Why?"

Rónán tried to hide his fear but knew the slight tremble in his voice betrayed him. "Well, I think… he… I sewed up the hole in his shirt," Rónán stuttered, a slight question in his voice. "Maybe he needs something else fixed?"

Douglas stared at him. Something about the cold, icy blue eyes made Rónán feel as if Douglas could see into his head, reading his thoughts about Abel. The knot in Rónán's throat was a knot of shame.

"Leave him be," Douglas barked. "Stay away from my brother." As he said the last word, he spat onto the ground as if punctuating his command.

Rónán didn't say anything. He nodded, casting his eyes to the ground. When Douglas turned back toward the porch, Rónán continued walking. He could feel the eyes of the other three on his back as he crossed the road and entered the grassy alleyway. Just as he reached his back door, thunder rumbled loudly overhead.

Once inside, Rónán closed the door and locked it. The latch clicked definitively. He put his back against the door and started to hyperventilate. He ran through questions in his head. What did Douglas know? Had Abel told him how Rónán was acting? Could he see the way Rónán looked at Abel—thought about Abel? The possibilities spiraled in his brain.

Rónán began to tremble. The shaking started in his hands and worked its way throughout his body. Another clap of thunder made him jump. His palms were sweating, and he was gripping the purple coneflower so hard that some of the leaves were crushed. In his anxious state, Rónán did not check his mother's notes again. Instead, he walked up the stairs to his room and began boiling a small tin of water, the same one he had used to make coffee just a few days ago. When the water popped with bubbles, he ripped up two of the flowers—roots, stems, petals, and all—and threw them into the pot. He snuffed out the flames of the cookstove and waited for his tea to steep.

When he felt the water had cooled enough, he scooped a mugful from the pot and cradled it in his hands. He hadn't even bothered to wash the plants, so a slight, muddy hue mixed in with the light chartreus shade of the tea. He sniffed at the cup, and a pine scent tickled his nose. Raising the cup to his lips, he sipped the brew, surprised to find that it had a floral flavor, along with an earthy bitterness. Rónán wondered if it would taste better had he only boiled the soft petals. As he sipped his tea, his mind kept returning to his interaction with Douglas. He felt an emptiness in the pit of his stomach that the brew could not fill. After a few minutes, he felt himself grow calmer. Was it his imagination or had his mother's directions worked? The scratchiness at the back of his throat was gone. He popped his knuckles and flexed his joints. They no longer ached.

Despite beginning to feel better, his hands continued shaking, setting off ripples in his cup as he sipped the final dregs of tea.

Wanting to quiet the noise in his head, he decided to get back to work on Helene's dress. Back in the shop, he sighed, trying to remember where he left off the night before. When he found a place to begin again, he turned his attention to the dress and began to work.

Chapter 8

A few hours later, as Rónán hunched over his sewing table, a light pattering, like the sound of chicken feet running across dry dirt, sounded from outside, beyond the window. Rónán pulled the curtain back an inch to see out. Percussive walls of rain dimpled the churning waters of the bay. He heard distant echoes of reverberating thunder. Knowing it did not take long for a storm to head inland, he hurried to the back door that led to the alleyway. The butcher's laundry was still on the line, and he did not want to have to launder again. Besides, he did not want to further anger Douglas.

As the door creaked open he heard a familiar voice.

"You know, Douglas wouldn't be happy if his aprons were returned all wet. I mean, he isn't usually happy anyway, but this would be a particular thorn in his eye."

Abel sprawled on the wooden steps leading up to the door. Rónán would have tumbled over him had he not been paying attention. The sight of Abel frightened him

"Does Douglas know you're here?" Rónán spat out.

Abel ignored his question and Ronan's obvious worry.

"I was wonderin' when I'd see you again," Abel laughed. "I was startin' to think you were avoiding me on purpose."

Rónán stepped around him and began retrieving the laundry from the clothesline.

"Were you?" Abel asked, his tone facetious, "Avoiding me, that is."

"I've… been busy," Rónán struggled to pick the right word.

"Busy?" Abel asked, unbelieving. "I know you've been workin' on that gown for Helene, but what else have the ladies of Bridewater got you doin' to keep you so busy?"

Rónán did not reply. He continued busying himself with his work, not looking at Abel.

After a moment, Abel pushed himself up off the stairs. Rónán noticed his shirt slowly darkening with the pelting rain that fell heavier and quicker now.

Rónán rushed to remove the last of the laundry, and holding the wicker basket on his hip like it was a child, made his way back to the door. He finally looked at Abel.

"Come inside," he said. "There's no use in you sitting out here in the rain."

Abel followed Rónán inside and shut the door behind him. His eyes lingered on the painted flowers for a moment. Rónán heaved the basket onto the front counter. Placing both of his hands on the flat surface on either side of the basket to steady himself, he continued looking down. They stood in silence for a moment, with only the hum of heavy rain between them.

Abel was the first to speak. "Listen." He sighed.

Rónán started to shake his head, already wanting to block this conversation.

"About the other night," Abel continued. "I'm sorry for messin' with your mom's stuff, I just—"

"What?" Rónán interrupted, confusion spreading across his face.

"No, I shouldn't have touched it. I can see that it brought up some—" Abel wasn't quite sure what it brought up but stumbled on. "Memories."

Rónán was speechless. That time was one of the few times memories of his mother had felt good rather than immensely sad. He continued looking down, not wanting to meet Abel's gaze.

"Rónán, I'm sorry," Abel finally said through the drumming of the rain on the windows. "Let me make it up to you."

Now, Rónán did look up, a question in his eyes.

"Supposin' it stops rainin'," Abel gestured toward the windows. "Let's go back to the pond. Just you and me."

When Rónán didn't say anything, Abel continued, "I don't have work tomorrow, and Douglas is busy with the shop. Clementine is going to her parents' for the day, and *you*," he gestured towards Rónán, "could use a break." Abel grinned in that charming, boyish way he had about him.

"Fine," Rónán said with a stifled smile. "If I can get through–"

"No 'if's'" Abel interrupted, laughing. "We are goin'."

"All right." Rónán was still trying to hold back his grin. "We'll go."

Abel punched the air in excitement, "First light?"

Rónán nodded, the smile now fully blooming on his face, but a sudden clap of thunder caused them both to jump and look toward the window. Abel laughed, and clapped Rónán on the shoulder.

"That was a big one," Abel said, raising his eyebrows. "If that ain't an omen? I better get goin'."

Thunk.

A sound came from above them. Their eyes shot to the ceiling.

Thunk.

The sound punctuated the tension in the room again. It was soft but definitive, like someone dropped a bag of apples on the floor above them. But the sound was familiar to Rónán. With a sharp intake of his breath, Rónán listened to the sound of the woman walking.

"Do you hear that?" Rónán whispered, wanting confirmation for once that he wasn't crazy.

"What is that?" Abel asked, but it wasn't the footfalls above he was asking about.

The sound of the bride's whispers seeped through the floorboards above, like a bathtub overflowing. Rónán attempted to shake the fright from his hands, but Abel chuckled.

"Who you got hiding up there, tailor? A pet snake?" he teased. "Is there someone in your room, horn dog?"

Abel bounded across the room and up the stairs, calling out, "'*elene*! '*elene*! *Get down 'ere zis instant*!" His voice mimicked Hector Hebert's Creole accent.

"No!" Rónán shouted. "Don't!"

Abel's foot stopped in mid-air above the bottom step. He looked back at Rónán, confused. His laughter faded away.

"Hey, now," Abel said calmly. "You alright?"

Abel could see the fear lining Rónán's face now. Rónán's eyes were wide, staring up at the ceiling. His mouth hung open, and he was quivering.

"Hey, hey, it's okay," Abel cooed. "Look, I can go up there and check it out, and–"

"No," Rónán interrupted. "Please. It's *her*."

"Her?" Abel asked. "Her who?"

"The bride," Rónán choked.

"Rónán, she's not real. It's just a story," Abel said. His voice held comfort rather than mockery.

Thunk. Thunk. Thunk. The walking started again.

Abel looked up, "Maybe that orange cat always hanging by my coops got inside or somethin'."

Rónán shook his head. The whispering in the room grew louder, crashing like waves against the walls. The trembling in Rónán's hands intensified. He brought his hands up to cover his face. Abel crossed the room to him, placing a hand on Rónán's back.

"It's alright," he said. "Listen, why don't I stay here tonight? We can sleep right here." And he gestured to the floor of the shop. As if she was the one being comforted, the bride's whispering stopped.

Slowly Rónán lowered his hands. He said, "I can't ask you to do that."

"You're not asking; I'm offerin'," Abel said. The footsteps overhead quieted. Without another word, Abel moved about the workroom, grabbing odd bits of fabric to fold them each a pillow. "It's hot enough," he continued, "I don't think we need any blankets anyway."

The boys settled into their makeshift beds on the floor. They slept facing opposite directions, Abel's head toward the stairwell and Rónán's toward the front door, the lamp between them. Its dancing flame cast wobbling shadows on the ceiling. They lay there for what seemed like an hour before Abel broke the silence.

"You know, my momma used to tell me stories about a creature that lived out in the bayou," he began. "The rougarou–a big ol' mean thing. Momma said it was ten feet tall, had the body of a man, the head of a wolf, and glowin' red eyes. It would eat people's cows and steal away misbehaving children."

Rónán remained quiet, listening.

Abel continued, "Anyone who saw it would be cursed. I used to stay up at night terrified that I'd wake up and hear that thing scratchin' on my windows."

When Rónán still didn't say anything, Abel leaned up on his elbows.

"Look," Abel said. "I'm sorry. Maybe that's not the best story to tell you right now, but I just want you to know, I know what it's like to be scared."

Rónán pushed himself up, meeting Abel's gaze, "But you were a kid."

Abel laughed, "Well, why do you think I hate walkin' home in the dark?"

Rónán allowed himself a small smile. "Thanks," he said.

"My pleasure," Abel said, then with a higher pitch in his voice, he continued, "Say, tell me about that green door. Did you paint all those flowers?"

"I painted them with Ma," Rónán said. "When I was little."

Abel propped his face on one hand to listen to the story.

"We painted it on Dad's birthday," Rónán continued.

"That sounds fun."

"Actually, I never knew my dad." Rónán saw the look of embarrassment on Abel's face, but he shook his head. "Don't worry. It happened a long time ago. His name was Tadhg. Ma always told me that she got her love of storytelling from him. He had a tall tale for everything."

Abel looked at Rónán intently. The flame between them flickered in his eyes, giving his irises a dark, amber hue.

"He was a sailor," Rónán continued. "Somehow that brought them to Bridewater. On the day we painted the door, Ma told me how they met. When she was a girl in Ireland, Ma lived in a village near the coast. One day, after her ma—my grandma—scolded her, she ran out the door and up the hills along the coast. She walked all day, just watching the ocean. Eventually, she saw a lighthouse and started toward it. As she did, she came across a boy with white-blonde hair–"

"Your daddy?" Abel asked.

"Yes, my dad." Rónán confirmed. "Well, the boy, my dad, bet her that he could beat her in a race to the lighthouse. As they were running—Ma always swore Dad was letting her win—Ma slipped on a rock and fell, tearing a big hole in the skirt of her dress."

Abel stared intently at Rónán. The candlelight cast shadows on his face.

"Dad stopped running and turned back to her, but Ma got mad. It wasn't really because of the dress though. At this point, she already knew how to sew. It's just, Ma was already in trouble with her ma, so she waited for Dad to come closer. When he reached down to help her up, Ma pushed him hard, making him fall against the rocks, too."

Abel threw his head back laughing. "She did what? And your Dad still married her?"

Rónán laughed, too, "Ma always said the one thing she never forgot that day was the green of Dad's eyes looking up at her all sad from her betrayal. For years they would meet at the lighthouse, and eventually—"

"Eventually, they got a *little seal*," Abel finished for him with a sly smirk.

"Yes, they did."

"Well, don't you think about pushin' me down in the pond tomorrow. I've gotta look out for gators, not rocks," Abel teased. "Besides, I'm not gonna marry you anyway."

Embarrassment colored Ronan's face, but he realized there was nothing mean in Abel's tone. It was his usual, joking manner. Still, he tried not to think about the comment.

With a stretch, Abel let out a big yawn and settled his head onto his makeshift pillow. "Man, I'm tired. Goodnight, *little seal.*"

"Goodnight," Ronan replied.

Rónán lay back on the floor. He kept replaying the picture of his mother and father frolicking on the coastal green hills of Ireland. He smiled to himself. After a moment, Abel's rhythmic, whistling breathing told him that Abel had fallen asleep.

Rónán rolled to his side. In the dim lamplight, he could still make out the shape of Abel asleep beside him. Rónán watched Abel's chest rise and fall in synchronization with his breathing. Even now in the darkness, Rónán could still see that there was something purely joyful about this boy, something wonderful. The feeling made him blush again.

Thunk.

Is she moving again? Ronan's stomach twisted, and that familiar, sour bile bubbled in his throat. He peered up through the cracks in the floorboards above him, half expecting a stitched eye to peek back at him. Did the bride stir only when his thoughts turned toward Abel? Was she angry at him for that? *But, no. I don't have the same feelings for Abel anymore.* Why would she punish him for just enjoying time with Abel?

Rónán forced his eyes closed, clenching his fists at his side to stop them from shaking. He needed to sleep. He tried to block out images of the drowned, rotting woman waiting for him in his bedroom, but every time he thought he was free from her, or he thought of Abel, another footstep sounded above. Somehow, despite his fear, exhausted, he fell asleep.

*   *   *

The sound of the tailor shop bell woke Rónán.

"Mornin', sunshine!" Abel said cheerfully, the fog of sleep still in his voice.

"Good morning," Rónán replied.

"I ran home to get us some food in case we get hungry." Abel held up a white bag that resembled a pillowcase. "I didn't know what you liked, but I figured this was better than nothin'. I had to get in and out of there quickly before Douglas got up, so I didn't spend much time lookin' for something. I thought I heard him stir, so I ran out of there quick."

Abel held up strips of meat that Rónán knew had been cured in salt and vinegar.

"That's perfect," Rónán said. "Thank you."

Rónán grabbed a few items of his own, and the boys set out into the streets of Bridewater to head back toward the oxbow pond. As they walked past the white-steepled Baptist church, Abel reached back into his bag, producing a strip of the cured meat and taking a bite out of the top. He held the remainder of the stick of jerky out towards Rónán. Rónán, suddenly aware of just how empty his stomach was, accepted the stick and took a bite. The meat was smoky and delicious. He chewed it, savoring every salty bit.

"Don't let Douglas fool you," Abel said with a flourish. "It's all Clementine. She could serve you a frog on a log, and it would be gourmet."

Rónán laughed, the sound adding to the chirping of insects around them.

Abel led the way to the blackwater river, and the boys traipsed through the scratchy underbrush along the banks until they came to the area where they knew the river curved back on itself creating the oxbow pond just behind a row of bushes.

"After you," Abel said, as he helped create an opening for Rónán to crawl through.

Rónán came into the clearing, and returned the favor for Abel, who slowly emerged, parting the grasses and branches in his way.

"Did my shirt hold up this time?" Abel asked jokingly, half turning to look over his shoulder.

Though it was still early, the day was already hot, and the early morning sun shone white off the clear water of the pond. The soft drone of insects cut through the trees, providing them with a kind of natural music.

"Well, what are we waiting for?" Abel ripped his clothes off and streaked towards the pond. In a golden blur, he leapt through the air and landed with a splash. He surfaced quickly, throwing his head back and smoothing his sandy locks with his hands.

"Get in, tailor!" He shouted aiming a playful splash at Rónán.

Perhaps it was how tired he was, or how lonely he often felt. Or maybe it was the sudden, complete comfort he found in Abel's presence, but for the first time, Rónán was not scared. He was not bashful. As quickly as Abel had disrobed, Rónán took his clothes off and jumped into the water sending a wave crashing toward Abel. As his head crested from the water, they both laughed.

The day was exactly what Rónán needed. They spent hours in the pond, alternately floating, sunbathing, talking, and napping. At one point, they even ventured into the woods that ringed the pond, Rónán pointing out various foliage and teaching Abel what each was used for. After they hiked for what seemed like hours, they decided to return one more time to the water to cool off before heading back into Bridewater.

As Rónán floated in the water, he noticed a flock of birds in the trees above them. They weren't immediately apparent, but their shiny reflective feathers squirming between the green of the sunlit leaves drew his attention. Every now and then, they would chirp back and forth, like a group of ladies gossiping after church. What Rónán especially noticed was their eyes. The reflective pools of their black eyes looked like calm, still water, and he felt like each bird stared at him from the abyss. It was like walking past the open window of an empty house. You hoped nothing was there, but your eyes strained to look beyond the darkness to see just what might be looking back at you.

Reaching towards his bag on the flat rock at the edge of the pond, Abel retrieved another piece of the stringy, dried jerky. He tore it in half, offering Rónán one half. As Rónán reached to accept it, Abel's eyes darted down to a mark on Rónán's forearm.

"What's that?" Abel asked, nodding his head toward the scar.

There was something different about it. It was pink and raised, like any other scar, but it also had neat, parallel lines where the skin had been stitched back together.

"Oh," Rónán said, looking down at his own arm. "It's a scar."

"From what?" Abel questioned.

"When I was a kid," Rónán began, somewhat embarrassed. "I was helping my mom in the shop. She was working on something for Madame Hebert. I insisted on helping, and being the clumsy person I am, I nicked my arm with the scissors."

"Did no one ever tell you not to run with scissors?" Abel joked. "I thought that would be like rule one in a sewing shop."

Rónán gave a shy laugh and sent a small splash toward Abel.

"Ma sewed it up," Rónán finished with a shrug, looking at Abel.

A cloud seemed to pass over Abel. His expression changed, dropped into something between darkness and sadness.

"How do you do it?" Abel asked quietly.

Rónán had never seen his friend so serious, "What do you mean?"

"I mean, your momma—, your shop. How do you do it?" Abel looked down at the water, not meeting Rónán's gaze. "How do you spend your days alone?"

Rónán didn't quite know what to say. It's not like he had a choice in the matter. Eventually, he broke the silence. "I just… do."

Rónán suddenly felt as if each blackbird was watching them now, attentive to every word they spoke. The birds had gone quiet. He thought their dark eyes reflected his own insecurity.

Rónán heard Abel sniff.

"You know," Abel said, "after my momma and daddy got sick and died, I told myself I'd leave here. I'd get on one of the ships in Bridewater Bay and never look back."

Abel began to cry.

"I never wanted to work at the docks," he continued, his voice quiet, his usual boisterousness gone. "I don't even know what I want to do, but I don't think Douglas would ever let me leave. He doesn't need me—hell, I don't even think he wants me. But it doesn't matter. You do what Douglas says or you don't do anything at all. But Clementine—I can't…" he trailed off.

Rónán was vaguely aware that the birds no longer shuffled along the branches or puffed up their feathers. They seemed as transfixed in this moment as Rónán.

"I know how you feel," Rónán sighed. His quiet added to the new stillness of the pond. Then he felt himself tearing up.

He spoke. "I've been scared every day since Ma left. I think part of me just continued her work thinking she'd come back some day. I figured, if I kept sewing, if I kept running the shop, she could just pick up where she left off, and we could act like nothing happened."

Rónán was crying now.

"But that was almost ten years ago," He swiped at his tears and paused to consider his words. "About a year ago, I tried to end it."

"What? I…" Abel stuttered.

Rónán chose each word carefully, speaking slowly. "I hadn't spoken to anyone in weeks, so I swam out as far into the bay as I could, until I was too tired to keep going. And then, I… well, I waited."

"Rónán—" Abel began.

Rónán wasn't finished. "But no matter how far I went, no matter how tired I got, I just couldn't… I couldn't sink."

He let his words hang between them for a moment.

"I would lie back, waiting to go under, but somehow, I floated back to shore," Rónán's vision swam. "It was like the tide just carried me back, over and over."

An ache knotted his throat. He felt ashamed, embarrassed. He expected to look up and see Abel disgusted by his crying. Instead, he found his friend's gaze held something else. It wasn't pity. It was something warmer.

Abel seemed to be considering his words.

"I'm just so glad you're here, *little seal*," he said, wiping away one of Rónán's tears with his thumb.

A sudden urge rippled up through Rónán. His skin felt electrified where Abel's flesh met his own. A spark ignited in his head. Surprising himself, he brought his lips to Abel's, pulling their faces together in a salty kiss. But as quickly as the urge came over him, Rónán pushed himself away from Abel, horrified at what he had done.

"Abel," he said. "I am so sorry."

Abel only looked at him in silence, his face not registering any discernible emotion. Rónán worried that Abel might strike him across the face.

"Abel, I didn't mean to. Please, I–"

In an instant, Rónán felt a hand on the back of his head. Abel pulled him in, and they locked in an embrace, bare chests together. Rónán knew Abel could feel how wildly his heart was beating. Then, suddenly, the hummingbird burst from Rónán's chest. His arms and neck erupted in goosebumps, and warmth flowered in his face and groin.

Abel brought his lips to Rónán's, and they kissed in a fiery passion. He felt Abel's tongue caress his own. Another of Abel's hands felt its way to Rónán's back, sending a tingle along Rónán's spine. Rónán wrapped his arms around Abel's shoulders, feeling the hard, protective warmth Abel's arms offered. Abel gently began to explore the softness of Rónán's neck with his mouth, kissing every inch of milky, white skin, causing Rónán to shudder.

Time seemed to stand still. And everything around them seemed to grow quiet outside of the sounds of their own breathing. But then, a familiar noise cut through the space between them. Heavy footfalls and snapping twigs shot through the stillness of their space.

Chapter 9

Rónán jerked his head away from Abel. Over Abel's shoulder, he saw Douglas, emerging from the thick, dark undergrowth surrounding the oxbow pond.

"What the fuck do you think you're doing?" Douglas yelled. His words were cold, and his blue eyes shot a chill through Rónán's body.

Rónán's eyes darted to Abel's. For the first time, he saw fear creep across Abel's face, like a cloud passing in front of the sun. Instinctively, Abel lifted his hand and gently tapped the bruise that puffed beneath his eye, now faded to green and yellow.

Rónán suddenly understood. The black eye, the pain, Douglas had caused it. Abel's hand betrayed his own secret.

"Douglas," Abel stammered. "I—" His thought hung suspended in the air.

Rónán felt scared but also determined to protect his friend. He pulled himself onto the flat rock near the pond, not even bothering to cover his naked body. He approached Douglas cautiously.

"Douglas," he said calmly, placing his hand on the butcher's forearm "It was—"

Before he could finish his thought, Douglas punched Rónán hard in the gut. Rónán fell onto the rock. The pain in his stomach was so intense he could feel bile rising in the back of his throat.

He lay on the rock, trying to catch his breath, he heard the slosh of water next to him as Abel rose from the rock. Whatever trance of fear that had paralyzed Abel a moment ago must have broken. He knelt down, touching Rónán's cheek with his palm.

"Are you alright?" Abel asked.

With a jerk, Douglas wrenched Abel's head backwards. He gripped a shock of Abel's sandy hair, giving the impression that tendrils of hair sprouted between his fingertips.

Yanking him forward, Douglas pulled Abel across the rock. Abel struggled to stay upright, tripping over his feet. When they reached the ash tree, Douglas kicked Abel to the ground, then shoved him against the tree so hard that the rough bark punctured the skin of his bare back. Using his left hand, Douglas pulled Abel's arm up and over his head, twisting it into an unnatural position. He used his knee to pin Abel's neck to the tree, causing Abel to choke and spit as he tried to yell. Abel tried to turn his head slightly but struggled under the weight of his brother. He was stuck there, painfully and oddly angled, looking up at his brother in a bastardization of forced reverence. With his right hand, Douglas reached into his front pocket and unsheathed a meat cleaver, gripping the wooden handle. Rónán struggled to his feet. The vomit rose to his chest, threatening to spill out, but he ran to the ash tree. With all the strength he could muster and despite his own pain, Rónán gripped Douglas' wrist, and struggled to grasp the knife handle. But Douglas pushed him away as easily as a horse bucking its rider. Douglas brought the butt of the knife handle down on Rónán's face, splitting open his skin.

Rónán fell back, hitting his head on the rock. His ears rang and his vision swam white. He tried to focus but could only catch glimpses. Douglas had quickly re-pinned Abel to the tree. Abel pleaded with his brother, but his words were suffocated by the knee on the back of his neck.

Douglas looked at Abel. His usually cold and expressionless face showed an unyielding harsh and ruthless hatred.

"I will not have a sodomite living under my roof." Douglas spat, so quiet he was almost whispering.

In a swift arc, Douglas brought the cleaver down, smashing into the ash tree in a heavy thunk. It slashed directly through Abel's fingers, severing his pinky and ring finger. Abel screamed, as raw, dry pain consumed him.

Rónán tried to understand what he had just witnessed. He saw Abel's fingers lying on the ground, as if they were bits of wood sawn from a tree. He saw the bloody stumps on Abel's hand.

Abel fell in a heap to the ground as Douglas released his grip. He pulled his bloody hand to his chest, holding it with his uninjured hand. He let out an anguished sob, and Rónán could see him shaking.

Douglas turned around, his expressionless face fixing on Rónán. He looked down at him, like a child looking down on an ant he was about to squish. The first kick connected with Rónán's chest. He felt and heard the wet crack of bone beneath his skin. He tried to move, but he was frozen. He knew what was coming, and he accepted his fate.

But before Douglas could strike Ronan again, a sudden blur of movement sent Douglas careening to the side. He and Abel tangled in a bloody, muddy heap.

"Go!" Abel screamed. *"Rónán leave!"*

As the brothers wrestled, Rónán strained to push himself up to his feet. He began tottering towards the brothers. Every inch he moved was painful. It felt like each step drove a thorn into his foot.

With his in-tact hand, Abel landed a punch square on Douglas' jaw, sending the older man staggering backwards. With the brief reprieve he had from the fight, Abel gripped both of Rónán's forearms, leaving bloody impressions of his remaining fingers on one.

The boys looked at each other. Pain, fear, and longing hung between them.

"Go!" Abel shouted.

"I'm sorry," Rónán cried.

"Go!" Abel repeated.

Douglas pushed himself to his feet and Abel turned back to face him.

Without gathering his clothes, Rónán began limping from the clearing. He was scared to leave Abel and scared of what Douglas might do. But he knew he was no match for the bigger man, and neither was Abel in his injured state. If he could only get back to town, he might be able to find help. He moved as quickly as he could, but every step brought additional pain—the pain from leaving his friend behind. In the near darkness, he found the blackwater river and began following it back to Bridewater.

He didn't know how long he walked or how exactly he managed to find his way back to the dirt roads of Bridewater through the fog in his mind. Eventually, the church greeted him. He stumbled into the graveyard, trying to call for help, but his voice was hoarse, broken with pain, and he could barely whisper. His foot slipped on the wet grass by one of the ornamental stones, and he fell to his hands and knees, the movement sending his head spinning in dizzying circles. He tried to reach out, to grab anything to right himself, but his hands only met the open air. His vision darkened, and he couldn't see more than a few inches in front of his face. He tried again to yell for help, but his brain was lost in a fog. No sounds emerged. He pushed his palms into the ground trying again to stand, but he didn't have the strength. The pain surging throughout his body was finally too much. His head fell to the ground, hitting a tombstone on the way down. He lay in the graveyard, bare stomach in the wet grass, his head to one side, looking up toward the black sky. The last thing he saw before succumbing to his pain was the bright, white moon staring back at him.

Chapter 10

Douglas rubbed his jaw with one hand, as if to massage away the pain from where Abel made contact. He spat on the rock between them. His cool blue eyes seemed devoid of emotion, but his face was contorted in a fiery rage.

"You're gonna regret that, boy," he said to Abel, taking heavy, stomping steps in his direction.

The pain in Abel's left arm made all movement feel as if he were jamming himself with a branding iron, but he tried to stand firm against his brother's approach. Douglas moved slowly, menacingly toward him.

"I should have drowned you when daddy died," Douglas said with venom. "Momma was always too soft on you—teaching you music, treating you like you were some porcelain doll."

Abel tried to keep his consciousness ahead of him, but the pain in his body made every movement feel like a shock. He held eye contact with Douglas, wanting to keep him moving toward him, hoping in the back of his mind that Rónán had left.

"After everything I've done for you all these years, you still have the gall to turn out like some queer," Douglas roared.

"Everything you've done for me?" Abel yelled, a laugh almost breaking through his anger. He started edging closer to the water. "Do you mean how you've hit me? How you've abused me?"

If this made Douglas angrier, he didn't show it. He just kept moving toward Abel, his hulking frame getting closer and closer.

"How you've hurt Clementine?" This seemed to spark something in Douglas. A flicker of anger darkened his eyes. "You think I don't see it? You think I don't hear her cry? See the bruises on her neck?"

"Shut your mouth!" Douglas screamed, spit flying from his mouth.

Abel shuffled closer to the water. "What would her daddy think? Would pastor——"

"I said shut your mouth!" Douglas roared, now sprinting toward Abel. At the last possible moment, Abel ducked out of the way, and Douglas fell headfirst into the chilly water.

Abel clutched his injured hand to his stomach and, without stopping for his clothes, sprinted into the trees. Without turning back, he heard Douglas pull himself out of the water, cursing behind him. Abel was becoming lightheaded from the blood pouring from his hand. In his confusion, he didn't know which way to run, only that he needed to put as much distance between himself and Douglas as he could. As he sprinted in the growing darkness, Abel ran through the thick undergrowth, limbs reaching out to scratch his exposed skin along his face and legs. He could hear Douglas crashing through the trees behind him, and he tried to pick up speed.

"Abel," Douglas' voice echoed through the trees, "Come back here now!"

Abel continued running. The muck at his feet made it difficult, but he had nowhere else to go but away from Douglas. He pushed past gnarled branches and felt thorns pierce his flesh. Every step he took felt like stepping into hot coals. His injuries rattled with each footfall. The sounds behind him quieted. Abel looked over his shoulder. It was nearly black in the trees now, but for the faint light of dusk.

His head was pounding and his breath rapid. He needed to stop. He leaned against a rotting, blackened tree to steady himself. His vision swam with lights and colors. He used his right hand to grab a branch for support. He tried to quiet his breath, hoping beyond hope that Douglas wouldn't hear him.

Through the trees ahead, Abel saw movement, something slinking in the shadows. Something about the silhouette didn't look natural. It was big, too big to be Douglas. Besides, he would have seen Douglas pass him, wouldn't he?

Abel squinted in the darkness, trying to bring the image into focus. The silhouette of the figure seemed fuzzy, like looking at it through a fogged mirror. The thing turned its head, revealing a long snout.

Bear, Abel thought. He knew black bears roamed here. It was turned to face Abel. In the darkness the creature lowered itself to all fours and started huffing, angling its nose towards Abel. As the bear moved closer, Abel knew from its desperate snuffling sounds that it was bound to reach him.

Abel stood still, paralyzed with fear, hoping the animal would give up if it didn't glimpse movement. He tried to quiet the heartbeat pounding in his ears. But he knew the sickly smell of blood that clung to him would attract any predator. He heard the crunching of wet leaves and snapping of fallen branches as the thing moved closer. His head was unsteady, still fighting the dizziness from his blood loss. He was about to make a run for it, sprint back into the unknown darkness surrounding him, when he felt a hand grip the back of his neck.

"You thought you could get away from me," Douglas said in a low, almost inaudible voice. He wrenched Abel's head back, forcing Abel to look him in the eye. Abel heard the creature running away, crashing through the trees. Blinded by his anger, Douglas did not seem to notice it.

"We are going home. Now. And you are going to forget about all of this nonsense," Douglas spat at him.

"Let go of me." Abel bucked wildly, trying to free himself.

"Let go!"

The more Abel squirmed, the tighter Douglas gripped his neck. Abel feared the cartilage in his neck would break from the pressure of Douglas' fingers. He was desperate, like an animal with its foot caught in a trap. He jammed his left hand with its bloody stumps into Douglas' eyes, painting his brother's face with slick, red blood.

In shock, Douglas let go of him. Abel tried to run, but the throbbing in his head began to overtake him as he stumbled through the trees. Douglas caught him in just a few steps. He grabbed his brother by both shoulders and turned him around, so they faced each other.

"You *will* come home with me now," Douglas growled at him. "You'll never see that little tailor boy again."

Abel took several ragged breaths. Looking Douglas in the eye he managed to say, "I hate you."

Douglas didn't respond.

"Momma and Daddy would hate you, too," Abel choked out.

Douglas grabbed Abel's chin with his right hand and yanked him so close they were only an inch apart now.

"I said," Douglas began coolly, "shut your mouth." He punctuated every word with a slight jerk of his hand, shaking Abel's head.

Abel looked at Douglas and spat square in his face.

Douglas' body heaved. In one swift motion, he brought the cleaver up from his front pocket and slashed it across Abel's neck, tearing a deep red gash. A violent red spurt of blood splashed across Douglas' face and onto the trees behind him. The shock of the blood awakened something in Douglas. For the first time, his eyes seemed to soften and he seemed surprised by his own action. Abel's eyes grew wide. He tried to breathe, but a gurgling sound filled his ears.

"Abel!" Douglas breathed. "Abel!" That was all he could say.

As the two men faced each other, Abel's face filled with shock and blood poured from his neck, splashing down his front and onto Douglas' shirt.

Douglas was horrified. He let go of Abel, allowing him to sink to the ground. Douglas said nothing more. Breathing heavily, he started to walk away from his brother, leaving him to die beneath the trees.

Abel desperately tried to hold the wound in his neck together. All he could think now was that he must get back to Rónán. Abel tried to stand and fell over. He tried to grab ahold of the trunk of the nearby tree, but his hands couldn't find purchase, and he fell again. Abel began crawling, not toward anything in particular, just away from this spot toward help. He tried again to push himself to his feet and managed to barely balance, swaying widely.

For what seemed like miles, he stumbled through the darkness. Somehow, he found himself back in the clearing at the pond, where he saw his and Rónán's discarded clothing.

Rónán, he thought.

Abel moved towards his clothes, but his legs grew weaker and his breathing more labored. He managed to reach the flat rock and fell hard to his knees, sending a jolting pain to his hip. Still trying to hold his neck in place, he tried to speak, to call for Rónán, but all that came out was a wet gurgling and spurts of thick, hot blood. He fell onto his back, his head slamming into the rock that was somehow still warm from the heat of late afternoon.

He lay on the rock looking up through the canopy of trees. He could barely see the moon, full and bright. The light seemed to dim as his vision faded. He willed himself to stay awake to no avail. His hands grew weak and fell to his sides, and he felt the cut across his neck open for a last time, sending blood running down his body, pooling beneath him on the rock.

With his last breath, he tried to call to Rónán, but he didn't even have the energy to form his name. The moon dimmed and faded to black. And then, there was nothing.

Chapter 11

Rónán awoke with a start. The gritty taste of mud caked his mouth. From the position of the moon, he could tell that hours had passed while he lay in the cemetery. He was worried for Abel, but certainly Abel would have returned to town by now. *Hadn't he?* He pushed himself up, gasping and aching, and walked straight toward the waters of the bay.

In the shallows, he began to sob. The moonlight's reflection on the surface of the water showed a young man he did not recognize. His hair was pasted to his face by blood, mud covered most of his body, and a small gash on his cheek leaked something dark.

With a shudder of pain, Rónán lowered his nude body into the water. He washed himself clean, sending out red and brown ripples from his body. He cried, his tears mixing with the saltiness of the bay.

After what felt like an eternity, he emerged from the water, not bothering to cover his nakedness, and walked back to the tailor shop. He found the spare key he kept hidden beneath a loose plank on the porch. The familiar doorbell greeted him. Without much thought, he picked up a needle and thread that sat on his worktable and with difficulty made his way up the stairs to his bedroom.

There he sat at his mother's vanity. Without any alcohol to clean or numb him, he began to stitch the wound on his cheek.

As he snipped the thread after pulling the final stitch through, Rónán looked into the mirror. His eyes were puffy and red, and bruises splotched the skin of his face, abdomen, and chest. But, for the first time, he felt like he was truly seeing himself.

All of his years alone had led to this. His time spent pining for the love that was missing in his life—his father, his mother, and friendships—brought him to this moment. Only now did he understand that he wasn't wrong for longing for a relationship with the father he never knew. He wasn't wrong for missing his mother who had disappeared a decade ago. He wasn't wrong for loving Abel.

And he did love Abel.

Tears began to stream down his cheeks. But this time, he wasn't crying out of sadness. This was something else, something new.

It was cleansing. It was acceptance.

Through the silence that blanketed his room, Rónán heard her whispering. Rónán opened his eyes. As he gazed into the mirror, the bride looked back through her stitched eyes and veiled face. This time, Rónán wasn't afraid. Just as he saw himself reborn for the first time, he recognized her.

"Ma!" he cried.

Rónán turned to face her and slowly untied the bonnet strings that bound her hands together in front of her body. Gripping his shears again, he delicately, stitch-by-stitch, freed his mother from her bindings and clipped each thread that held her eyes and mouth closed. Gently he pulled the threads loose from her decaying skin, freeing her from her shackles.

As she opened her eyes for the first time in a decade, Aislyn saw her son, a young boy and a grown man all at once.

Rónán snipped the final thread at the edge of her mouth and Aislyn gripped her son in a hug. She brought her mouth to his ear, and her trickling whisper became a flood, submerging him in the explanations he had yearned for.

* * *

Something had drawn her attention down at the docks. As her eyes finally adjusted to the night, she'd seen formless shapes materializing from the darkness in the moonlight. A crumpled heap at the end of the dock, Hector Hebert, with his pants pulled down, exposing his buttocks, and the bride of Douglas the butcher.

"Clementine?!" she managed to gasp. "Hector, what is happening?"

But even in her disbelief, Aislyn knew it was something sinister. Clementine floated in and out of consciousness. Her gurgled cries called to Aislyn. The shopkeeper's thick, calloused hands gripped Clementine's throat, purple radiating out from where the man's fingers met her skin. His grip so tight that her blood stained his fingertips.

"Hector, what are you doing? Get off her!" Aislyn cried, mustering all her strength to grip the man's arms and free the trapped woman who was struggling to breathe.

But her strength was no match for the shopkeeper's. With the ease of swatting a fly, Hector backhanded Aislyn, sending her spinning toward the ground. The floral wreath she carried fell from her grasp, landing on the knotted wood of the dock. Aislyn gasped from pain, already feeling a warm trickle of blood running down from where the shopkeeper's hand had hit her cheek. Through the ringing in her ear, Aislyn could still hear the cries of Clementine. She stood again, silently praying for strength.

Again, Aislyn leapt upon the man, this time, digging the heels of her feet into the man's calves. She mustered every ounce of strength she could and grabbed Hector's arms to free the poor woman beneath him.

Aislyn screamed until her throat was raw.

This time, the shopkeeper turned his full attention to Aislyn, letting go of Clementine's neck and, causing a fit of ragged coughing. Hector elbowed Aislyn in the side of the head, knocking her off her balance and freeing him from her kicks. Then, he turned his full attention to her. His punch connected with her jaw. The force of the hit sent her bonnet flying from her head.

Aislyn heard the crack as his blow shattered her jaw. She felt the muscles in her face try to hold everything together but fail in a painful ripping beneath her skin. She fell backwards, hard. Her head bounced off the dock, sending lightning through her entire body. She could feel warm blood dripping from her nose, its metallic taste on her tongue. She strained to hold her eyes open to see the face of the man above her, framed by the stars. There was none of his usual warmth behind his eyes. She thought she was floating, but the pain kept bringing her back down to earth. It was unbearable.

The shopkeeper sent another kick directly to her abdomen. This time, the other woman tried to help.

Clementine had struggled to her feet and, with what little strength she had, tried to push the man off of Aislyn. But she was too weak from her own injuries and no match for his size. Hector pushed her aside, sending her into the oil slick waters of the bay.

Aislyn tried to speak. But she needed help. She was dying. Clementine was dying.

Hector showed no pity. Nothing crossed his face but rage. He lowered himself onto her, using his full weight to pin each of her arms to the dock and looked down at her. There was nothing in his eyes, not even hatred. Seeing the wreath beside her on the dock with its long line of thread leading from the needle, he gripped the needle and thread in his large, thick hands. With his left hand, he pinched her lips together.

"You won't say anything," the shopkeeper growled, stabbing the needle through Aislyn's lips. He pulled uneven, jagged stitches across her mouth, sewing her lips together.

"Because you didn't see anything." This time, as his left hand pinched her eyes closed, his right drove the needle through the thin layers of skin that formed her eyelids.

Aislyn tried to scream in pain as she felt the needle pierce the white jelly of her eye beneath her eyelid, but her screams were constrained by the stitches holding her mouth shut. Again, she could feel the blood, running like tears now, falling from her eyes. Every prick of the needle brought agony as the man perverted her craft, using it against her.

Standing, the shopkeeper picked up her bonnet. Aislyn felt him coil the fabric ties tightly around her wrists, binding her hands together. Hector knotted them so hard, that even amidst all the other pain, she could feel her wrists screaming, radiating a white heat up to her shoulders.

Unable to see what was happening, Aislyn felt him moving her. She was lifted and then felt herself falling. Once again, her head smacked against wood but this time, the surface beneath her moved. Amidst her confusion, the word "boat" came to her mind. She was dropped into the rowboat that docked in the bay.

Aislyn fought sleep. Though her head lay still, she struggled to bear the weight of it.

Her brain tried to make sense of what was happening. Aislyn couldn't see anything, but she could hear. The rhythmic splashing of the oars punctuated the sound of water lapping the side of the boat. Mingled with those sounds was the rattling breathing of the shopkeeper. He didn't speak to her.

After what felt like an eternity and an instant, the sound of rowing stopped. Aislyn perceived the boat rocking with the man's shifting weight. She felt his thick arms slide underneath her. Once again, she was lifted. Then, wordlessly, Hector dropped her over the side of the boat.

The saltwater entering her wounds burned. Her nose and the small slits of her eyes burned where the salt water managed to seep its way through.

Aislyn desperately kicked her feet, trying to keep herself right side up and afloat. But slowly, her waterlogged skirt pulled her down no matter how hard she fought against it. As her head dipped under the water, she tasted the brine through the small corner of her mouth that wasn't quite closed by the stitches.

Now she knew. There was no more hope for her.

A new image came to her mind. The burning saltwater became the burning of her son's red hair. The stars that still floated in her blackened vision became his freckles.

Rónán, she thought.

"Rónán," she repeated as best she could, sending tiny bubbles up from the small opening at the corner of her mouth.

A kind of peace came over her. She no longer felt she was drowning. Instead, she felt as if the bay was accepting her, cradling her, carrying her down to its soft sea floor.

As the sea pulled her down, she remembered what she had learned from her mother.

With the last of her energy, and with a calming peace washing over her, she repeated a charm of protection over herself and mentally recited it as her liturgy until she felt nothing.

As her words floated in the bubbles that trailed to the surface of Bridewater Bay, everything faded to black. Amidst the black, she saw a series of images illuminated as if by the strike of a match .

First, an image of Clementine on the long dock in Bridewater Bay. Scrubbing away the blood that had soaked into the wood with a handful of salt and a brush.

Then, an image of her red-haired boy, looking out the windows of their home, day after day, night after night, year after year.

Then an image of her son, now a young man, walking the streets of Bridewater. Another flash of her boy, with a frightened look on his face, watching her from the window.

She saw herself walking toward him as he cowered under a blanket, saw herself slowly push his bedroom door open and stretch her arms out, wanting to comfort him.

In another flash she waited for him in his room, but he never came.

Finally, there he was, looking at her in the mirror. No longer scared. No longer avoiding her.

Chapter 12

Rónán cried. For the first time in a decade, he had answers. He cried because of the anger and hatred that burned in him for Hector. He cried at the town that failed him, allowed him to live alone and neglected though he was only a child. He cried because of the sadness he felt for his mother, the woman who served this town, who only existed to heal and create—murdered and cast aside like rotten meat. He cried because he had left the person he loved at the pond with his abusive brother and now he wondered if Abel had survived. Rónán needed to find Abel and perhaps help him leave this place and Douglas and Bridewater for good. Rónán wanted to scream and run through the streets of Bridewater forcing his neighbors to hear what Hector had done to his mother, what Douglas had done to Abel. Pain was so familiar to him now. There was nothing he could do to extinguish his pain, so it might be better to just let it burn.

Rónán looked at himself in the mirror. His mother was gone, no longer hugging his shoulders and whispering in his ears. The cut on his cheek and the wound near his scalp still oozed, so he washed himself again, the water in the porcelain basin turning pink. Without bothering to numb himself with the paste made from cloves, as his mother taught him, he grabbed a needle and thread and sewed the wound at his scalp. Each stitch reminded him of Hector and his mother and made him determined to make Hector pay for what he had done.

Gingerly, Rónán dressed himself. He sat cross legged on his floor, between his bed and the cookstove. He reached into the old wooden chest containing Aislyn's things, feeling for the familiar texture of her leatherbound diary. When he first came across it among her other books, reading it was too much to bear. He had thrown it into the box, locked it tight, and never looked back. But now, he read.

It was as if he were a lamp that had been snuffed and suddenly lit again. As he read, years of memories, lessons, and stories rushed back—things he had forgotten about and things he had forced himself to forget. Throughout the night, Rónán rekindled his knowledge of his mother's magic. He read her descriptions of Ogham divination, how his ancestors read the stitches in a garment to try to interpret the fates before them, how they used their own power to stitch their prayers, charms, and wishes into fabrics with neat Ogham lines. This gift was his heritage.

When he came to an entry dated the day after his birth, he felt sick. *She knew she was going to die. She knew Rónán would be left alone.* He threw the diary against the room, as new grief spread in his body like a virus.

How could she leave me? He thought. Aislyn had lived for over nine years with the knowledge that someday, her son, her *little seal,* would be all alone in Bridewater.

Throwing his head back, he screamed to the heavens until his throat grew raw. He sobbed into his hands and thrashed about, hitting anything within reach.

When he stopped crying, Rónán crawled on his hands and knees to retrieve his mother's journal. He suddenly felt ashamed of his reaction, how he had abused one of his last possessions from his mother. The book opened to what appeared to be the final entry, dated just before her disappearance.

Rónán wiped his runny nose and began reading. This entry was not a journal entry. It was a letter to Rónán, dated just a few weeks before she disappeared. He could almost hear his mother's voice as he read:

October 13, 1887
My dearest, Rónán,

>   *I must start with an apology. In my own*
> *birthing bed, I saw my death foretold. For over*
> *nine years now, I've walked Bridewater with this*

knowledge as my dark shadow. I have let it grieve me more than I can say. After your father died, I did not think I could go on. When I divined that I, too, would die, I had no choice. But how can I prepare my boy for his mother's death when he's already lost so much? I thought about sending you home to Ireland to live with your grandmother, but I know now that I cannot. Just as I've seen my own fate, I've seen yours. I see that you are made for something big, something even I cannot yet comprehend, something laid in the very stitches of the curtains hanging in your room. I see you bringing life to your work. All I can hope now is that through this book, you remember exactly who you are and who came before you. I am again sorry that I will one day leave you but know that I am never truly gone. I will still whisper to you in the wind and sing to you in bird song. I will be the butterfly that kisses your cheek and the eye that watches you always. You are perfect in every way that you are and every way that you will be.

I love you so much, my little seal.

Forever yours,

Your mother, Aislyn

Tears ran down Rónán's cheeks as he squeezed his eyes shut. He swallowed hard, trying to dislodge the knot in his throat. His breaths steadied. For maybe the first time in his adult life, Rónán found himself with a sense of purpose. He was still intensely worried for Abel but knew what he needed to do. Before he could leave Bridewater, he had work to finish.

* * *

Before the sun's first rays filled the room, Rónán picked up where he left off working on Helene's dress. He manipulated and draped the rich, mauve fabric into the perfect silhouette, and he sewed. Only now, his craft felt different. He wasn't just connecting pieces of fabric together, he was using his mother's lessons. He was following all of her lessons, not just the ones involving pulling a needle and thread through cloth, but the lessons that went beyond that, that went into memory and magic. He pulled seams of protection, luck, and love through the dress in the Ogham letters, all the while muttering his own song-like prayers into the threads of the gown. Somehow, his craft felt cleaner, lighter, quicker. He did not stop working until well into the evening. When the light inside the shop finally grew golden in the setting sun, he finished. He stood back to admire his work. Before him on the mannequin hung an elegant-but-casual gown that Helene could wear every day.

Not wanting to leave any loose ends, Rónán folded the dress neatly and packed it into a box, lining the edges with a light, flimsy paper he typically used to make patterns. He reached below the counter to retrieve a corked bottle and stuffed it into his front pocket along with the folded leather pouch that held his spare needles and thread. With the box in hand, he started walking through the back alley toward the general store.

As he walked in front of the chicken coops, he heard a muffled angry conversation coming from inside the butchery, and, before he could react, the back door flew open. The orange cat that had been sunning nearby darted at the sound of the door. Clementine came flying into the alleyway, falling down the back stairs into a crumpled heap. Rónán saw the butcher framed by the doorway, looking down at them both. Even from a distance, Rónán could smell the woody, antiseptic smell of the whiskey emanating from his skin. There was nothing in his cold, blue eyes. He looked at Rónán and spat on the ground, daring him to speak. "Get out of here," Douglas slurred, slamming the door shut.

Rónán knelt, tucking the box under one arm and helped Clementine to her feet. "Are you all right?" he asked her.

Clementine brushed the front of her skirt with her hands, freeing the grass and dirt that clung to it. As she righted herself, she pulled the high collar of her dress over her neck, hiding the bruises that Rónán knew bloomed on her skin.

Clementine spoke. Her words were short, clipped, as if she was worried about being overheard. "Fine," she said quietly. "Tripped is all."

"Clementine, I—" Rónán began, but she shook her head no. Her small frame trembled like a scared rabbit, and she did not meet Rónán's gaze as she walked off toward the white steepled church that lay just beyond the alley.

"Clementine," Rónán called after her. *"I know."*

Her steps seemed to stutter as she registered his words, but she didn't turn back.

"I know… and I'm sorry," Rónán finished.

Rónán saw her right hand reach up to her face as though to wipe a tear away.

He felt like he finally saw Clementine for the first time. He realized that she wasn't just shy, she was scared. Like him, she had spent her life in this place full of painful memories. This place where neighbors knew her pain but only smiled at her without offering to help. Where she suffered in silence and isolation. Remembering his mother's account of what Hector did to Clementine, he vowed not to be like the rest of Bridewater. He wouldn't smile at someone's face only to whisper behind their back or wait in silence, ignoring others' screams. If he had the power to do something, he would.

Rónán approached the general store, and found the front door closed. The Heberts had already closed for the evening. He knocked. After a moment, he heard a soft padding of footsteps approaching the door. Helene opened the door, sounding the small bell overhead.

She smiled, "Good evening, Rónán. What can I–" She trailed off and her smile wilted as she looked Rónán up and down. He knew he must be a sight. His pale skin was mottled with bruises. Swollen, red stitches stood out on his cheek and hairline, and his lip was split in the middle.

"Maman? Papa?" Helene called hesitantly into the emptiness behind her, keeping her eyes on Rónán's swollen face.

"Don't worry. I'm all right, Helene," Rónán said, as if he could read her thoughts. "May I come inside?" He lifted the box in his hands to present it to Helene, wincing at the pain that jabbed between his ribs.

Helene's eyes lingered on Rónán as she stood aside for him to enter. He limped past her and stood in the main room of the general store, still clutching the box.

"If you don't mind," Rónán started, "could you try this on? I need to make sure it fits before you leave for school." He opened the top of the box, revealing the deep, mauve fabric within.

Helene's eyes widened, but she still seemed hesitant to approach Rónán, as if whatever misfortune that caused him to look like this might infect her. She held her arms out hesitantly, her eyes on Rónán's face. When she took the package, she retreated to one of the backrooms without a word. While he waited, Rónán looked at the products that lined the shelves. Just being in this space filled his mind with images of Hector on the dock with Clementine and his mother. He tensed.

After a moment, Helene reentered the room. She looked beautiful. The mauve gown made her dark skin glow and accentuated the rosy undertones of her cheeks. The dress hugged every soft curve of Helene's hips and chest, making her look like a grown woman. The few small flowers he had embroidered onto the bodice in a lighter lavender-colored thread he had modeled after ones Aislyn had expertly sewn into Helene's blanket all those years ago and emphasized Helene's natural beauty. For a moment, Rónán admired his work and admired the beautiful girl who made the gown look even more magnificent. Helene smiled, but an edge of worry lined her face as she modeled the gown for him. Caught up in his delight seeing how well his creation fit her, Rónán didn't hear the other sets of footsteps enter the room from the back hall.

Hector spoke first, the very sound of his voice sending acid to the back of Rónán's throat, "*Mon Dieu*! Rónán, what has happened to you?"

Henriette made a clicking noise with her tongue, reminding Rónán of a clucking hen. "*Cheri,* are you all right?" she asked, her sweet southern voice accented with worry. "Hector, get a chair, please."

He did not, could not look at Mr. Heber. Looking at Helene's mother Henriette, he replied. "I just came to deliver this and make sure it fits Helene," he said gesturing toward Helene who stood tentatively in her new gown.

Mrs. Hebert's face held a look of motherly worry. "Please, come sit."

Mr. Hebert carried a small stool that usually sat behind their front counter and set it beside Rónán, patting the cushioned seat as if inviting Rónán to sit. Now Ronan looked at Hector Hebert. He felt he was truly seeing him for the first time, like looking at a blurred photograph that suddenly comes into focus. It finally made sense why the man showered him with kindness in the absence of his mother and why Hector would never look Rónán in the eyes. For the first time, he could see the wary look of fear in Hector's dark brown eyes.

"Why did you do it?" he asked the empty air between him and Hector. "Why did you hurt my mother?"

Mr. and Mrs. Hebert looked at each other, something Ronan could not identify passing between them.

"What do you mean?" Henriette asked. "Please, child, let us help you. Your mother—she saved our Helene so long ago, and we have never forgotten. Let us help you. It is the least we can do."

Rónán slammed his fist into the seat of the stool that Hector placed before him. "Tell her!" he spat.

Hector, chuckling nervously, cast his gaze between Henriette and the top of Rónán's head. "*Mons fils*, you are confused. Take a seat, please."

In a swift movement that made Henriette jump backwards and Helene scream, Rónán struck Hector across the face with a resounding slap. Mr. Hebert's dark complexion went unusually, sickly pale. Something heavy crept over his brow as his eyes locked on Rónán's. A slow, thick trickle of blood leaked from the corner of his mouth.

Without freeing his gaze from Rónán, Hector spoke coldly, calmly. His accent seemed to dissipate, making his words sound unnatural, "Henriette, Helene—go upstairs. *Now.*"

"Dear—" Henriette started to say, but she was cut off.

"Now."

Henriette wrapped her arm around Helene's shoulders, and the two women walked to the back stairs. Helene looked back, her eyes worried.

Hector waited until the sounds of the two women faded. He took a deep breath, straightening his bowtie before speaking again. His voice was quiet but forceful and full of venom. "Listen, boy. I don't know what you're—"

"Don't lie to me!" Rónán erupted, his decade of anguish boiling over.

The two men looked at each other, and then as if he had been struck, Rónán began to cry, pleading, "Don't lie to me. Please."

Hector reached one broad hand up to flatten his mustache as he considered his next words. He spoke carefully, "Your mother meddled with something she ought not have meddled with. What happened was finished years ago. We don't have to get anyone else involved. End it."

A strange, numb feeling washed over Rónán, like his whole body had just received an electric shock and the ripples were still pulsing through him. He wiped his eyes with the cuff of one sleeve, "You don't want anyone else involved? Then come with me."

"Rónán, it's late," Hector started. "Go home. We can talk tomorrow after you've had time to cool off."

"You'll come with me," Rónán stared at him, not blinking, "or I'll go upstairs right now and tell your wife and daughter everything."

Hector considered a moment. His shoulders seemed to slump with the weight of Rónán's words.

He finally spoke, his voice gruff, almost a whisper, *"D'accord."*

They exited the general store walking in silence, Hector a few paces behind Rónán, until they reached the docks across from the tailor shop. The wood beneath them sagged with their weight as they walked toward the back of the dock. When they reached the end, Rónán faced Mr. Hebert.

"Why did you do it?" Rónán repeated, his voice eerily quiet against the sound of the waves. "Why did you take her from me?"

Rónán looked over the bay, watching the moonlight dance across the surface of the dark water, unable to think of anything else. He had seen the visions his mother had whispered, but he could not comprehend how anyone could hurt the loving, gentle, angelic woman. Rónán turned away from Hector and began to cry from frustration and sadness.

"Why did you—" but before he could finish his question, Hector knocked him over with a punch to Rónán's cheek. Rónán felt the warmth of blood as his stitches popped. His head, already aching from his wounds, screamed in agony.

Like a small child, Rónán tried to steady himself on his feet. The dock seemed to be buckling beneath him. Before he could find his footing, he felt another punch connect with his head, this time opening the stitches on his scalp, sending his vision swimming in red as blood from the reopened wound seeped into his eyes. Rónán fell and lay writhing, trying to keep his sight from going black.

In his strobing vision, he saw Hector waddling toward him. He flipped Rónán onto his back and began to pummel him.

"You're just like your momma, boy," Hector punctuated each word with a kick of his boot. "You don't know when to leave things alone."

Rónán felt one of his ribs crack and screamed in pain. He tried to stay focused, but the fiery pain seared through his body.

Hector stood over Rónán's writhing body, nothing but a dark shadow silhouetted by the moon in Rónán's dim vision. Hector leaned down getting so close that Rónán could smell the hint of peppermint on his breath as he spoke.

"I'm going to kill you just like I killed your momma, *mons fils.*" He got onto his knees, sitting on Rónán's chest, and leaned his face even closer, his saliva falling onto Rónán's face. Hector wrapped his large hands around Rónán's neck and started to squeeze.

Rónán saw stars. His vision, already fading, grew blurry with the expanding pressure on his eyeballs. In what he thought might be his last moments, visions of his life appeared blurry through the darkness. He saw his mother, laughing and smiling at him, a hint of music gleaming in her eyes. He saw Abel, his boyish, round eyes and playful grin. And then, he saw himself, alone in his shop, preparing for this moment. Rónán reached around, his hand fumbling in his front pocket.

Gasping, he managed to spit, "You'll never catch a good tailor without his needle." With that, he pushed a sharp, sewing needle into the center of Hector's right eyeball.

Hector pulled his hands back from Rónán's neck as if he received an electric shock and screamed in pain. Hands to his face he tried to pull out the needle, but his hands and the needle were so slicked with blood that he couldn't get a grip on it. Screaming Hector fell to one side, desperately clawing at his eyes.

Rónán coughed, hacking out a viscous, bloody mucus with each exhalation. His body heaved, but his stomach was so empty, nothing came out but foamy red bile. He pushed himself to his feet, swaying as he tried to stay upright. With one foot, he pushed Hector onto his back at the edge of the dock. Overcome by the sharp, stinging pain in his eye, Hector had stopped fighting back.

Rónán knelt down over the bigger man, and using his knees, pinned his arms into place against the dock. Then, he reached into his other pocket and pulled out a smaller, glass vial containing a murky, mossy liquid. His mother's journal held many lessons, and this was another. With one hand, Rónán grabbed Hector's lower jaw and forced it open. With the other hand, he poured the liquid, a concentration made from water hemlock and oleander, into Hector's mouth. Any minute now, the shopkeeper would lose consciousness and maybe start to convulse, but not before Rónán made him know pain.

Rónán's words were thick. He fought through pain and saliva to say them.

"You won't say anything," Rónán pushed a needle and thread through Hector's lips, pulling threads from between the dark bristle hairs of Hector's mustache. "Because you didn't see anything." One by one, Rónán stitched the shopkeeper's mouth and eyes closed.

Even now, straddled atop the heavy man's chest, his knees digging into Hector's arms, Rónán could remember sitting at his mother's heels. She would sit in her wooden chair, rocking, singing, and telling her son stories while she sewed. As Rónán dragged his needle through Hector's skin, embroidering another Ogham stitch dyed red with blood, he could hear his sweet mother, humming her charms, her melodies of protection, of love.

This was not protection. This was not love. This was retribution. This was penance. This was as Rónán willed.

Pain.

When he finished closing Hector's eyes and mouth, he severed the ends of the threads with his teeth to tie them off. With the remaining, bloodstained, fine strings, he brought Hector's hands together and wrapped them tightly, spooling the threads around his wrists hundreds of times, the tight, thin fibers digging painfully into the meaty flesh at Hector's joints. When Hector was bound in the same way he bound Aislyn, Rónán stood to examine his work. The shopkeeper heaved and kicked, but Rónán could sense the poison slithering through his muddy veins, like a mold spreading from his stomach. With a strength he didn't know he had, Rónán dragged the writhing man into the rowboat sitting along the edge of the dock. Hector's muffled cries tried to escape their bondage, but Rónán's work was too good, too clean, unlike Hector's own.

Rónán paddled out in the bay, seemingly aided by some invisible current. He went so far that he could no longer see the lone gas lamp at the mouth of the Bridewater docks. When he finally reached his destination, he knelt close to Hector again. The hemlock had taken over during the course of the trip, and the man was no longer moving, but his labored breathing showed that Hector was still conscious. He could still hear and feel.

"This was for my mother," he said. "I want her to be the last thing you think about as you die."

Without any more words, Rónán heaved the heavy man over the side of the boat. The splash sent the boat rocking, and Hector's body sank into the darkness, like dark hands had reached out from the depths to pull him into their eternal embrace. When the bubbles stopped popping along the surface, Rónán fell onto his back in the boat.

Chapter 13

Rónán stared at the sky. Behind him, a sliver of sun crested over the horizon, reflecting brilliant, deep orange over the surface of the bay, sending watercolor tendrils of purple and amber dancing across his vision. He breathed in deeply. Throbbing pain beat through his body. With every movement of his face, he could feel the dried blood cracking. Though he could not see the shore, Rónán stood and dived into the bay. A rush of cold made him gasp.

He cleansed himself in the waters, freeing blood and mud from his hands, face, and body. The cool water soothed his bruises, but the salt stung each cut it reached. Treading water, he turned over and floated on his back, allowing the current to lick his wounds.

As the sun grew brighter overhead, Rónán considered the last few days. For the first time in his adult life, he had answers. He knew his mother didn't just disappear and leave him behind. A decade's worth of sadness had been extinguished in one night through the visit from the soul of his mother, but another feeling within him could not be extinguished. As the sun warmed his face, an image of Abel, smiling, laughing, teasing, swam into his mind. He had to return to Bridewater to find Abel.

The old, wooden rowboat bobbed like a buoy in the bay. Being careful not to capsize the boat and panting from the pain and effort required, Rónán grabbed the oars. He looked down into the water. No gravestone would mark where the body of the man now laid. As he watched the waters bobbing and cresting in a white foam, he suddenly felt ill. He may have been freed from his curse, but he knew now that he had passed it to someone else. Henriette and Helene would sit with the pain of unanswered questions for the rest of their lives while everyone around them in Bridewater ignored their pain. Rónán cried, knowing this pain all too well and hated himself for perpetuating it.

Rónán began paddling back to shore, the water's current helping push him forward. As he approached the muddy shores, a few men were walking toward the docks ready to begin their day of work. No one seemed to notice Rónán bobbing out on the water. He ached from the effort of rowing. It was like any other day in Bridewater: the people lived their lives while Rónán struggled, just out of line of sight. He watched for a moment, hoping to see Abel's face among the men returning to work at the docks. He turned the boat away from the docks and paddled toward the line of mud and sand where the earth met the bay just east of the Baptist church.

Tying up the boat in a hidden patch of reeds, Rónán leapt into the knee-high waters and sloshed to the shore. He thought about limping to the Duvall Family Butchery, but the thought of Douglas made his stomach turn. Besides, he was sure that Abel would not be there.

Retracing the path they had taken twice before, Rónán made his way toward the meandering blackwater river that ran just outside of Bridewater. He followed every bend and twist until he came to the familiar, overgrown spot. Where he and Abel had pushed their way through to the oxbow pond, the brush was bent and twisted at odd angles. This must have been where Douglas stood watching them, hiding in the overgrown thicket, waiting to confront them.

Careful not to aggravate his injuries, Rónán moved into the clearing. He blinked at the sudden, bright light reflecting off the clear waters of the pond. When his eyes adjusted, he dropped to his knees screaming.

There on the flat rock next to the pool, Abel lay lifeless. He was on his back with his chest and face open to the sun, his legs and arms splayed at odd, unnatural angles. His usual warmth was gone. His eyes were open, but the joke in his head was forgotten. His hair no longer shone but was dull like an old penny. His skin looked pale, cold, and bruised. Rónán moved to Abel's side.

"Abel, please?" he cried, looking at Abel's face, his pale lips parted ever so slightly.

There, along the middle of his neck, a single line, deep, blackened red, ran where Douglas must have cut him. Dried blood the color of an aged port wine had collected on his neck and chest. Rónán clasped Abel's injured hand and brought it to his forehead. sobbing. There on the rock beside him lay Abel's severed fingers, like river reeds cut from their stalks. Next to them, Rónán saw the butcher's blood-stained cleaver reflecting the sunlight. Rónán picked it up and threw it into the water, letting out a guttural, primal yell.

Rónán looked around him. Their clothes still sat, carelessly disregarded on the rocks, as if they would return to them any moment. Carefully arranging Abel's body, Rónán laid his friend out. He even arranged the boy's severed fingers next to their rightful place on his hand. When he was done, Abel lay nude in repose.

Rising to his feet, Rónán scooped up his own shirt and approached the water's edge. Dipping the cloth into the cold water, he cleaned Abel's body. He gently scrubbed at Abel's skin, delicately dabbed at the corners of his eyes and mouth until they were clean and sponged the length of his body until even his muddy feet were clean. His tears mixed with the water as he worked. Repeatedly he dipped his shirt back into the water and wrung it clean, until every inch of Abel's skin was freed of grime. Except for the bruises, he looked like he was resting, dozing in the sun after a lazy summer dip in the pond.

Grief washed over Rónán again. He brought his forehead down to Abel's chest and he cried. He cried for what was, what could have been. His chest heaved and he rocked in anguish. He wanted nothing more than to lie here, his head resting on Abel's chest, to await his own death.

Rónán heard something behind him, like the sound of a fish leaping out of the water, but he didn't give it attention. He found himself holding Abel's hand again.

Behind him, it sounded as if someone lifted themself from the pond. Rónán rubbed Abel's forearm as if he could bring warmth back into his body. As Rónán knelt, he felt a dull jab in his upper thigh. Reaching into his front pocket, he felt the small leather pouch that carried his supplies. Inside, he found a small, silver needle.

Wet footsteps padded against the flat rock behind him. Rónán turned. There, standing on the rock before him was a young woman. His mother looked at him, no longer the bloated, bruised, and graying corpse, but the young woman he remembered. Her skin was smooth and pale, her hair fiery red in the sun, and her eyes deep, crystal blue and smiling.

Wordlessly, Aislyn approached her son. From behind, she hugged him and touched her soft lips to his cheek. She was warm, and Rónán felt her heat through every inch of his body. She smelled light and sweet, like a bouquet of lilies. Gently she threaded her arm through his. With their arms interlocked, Rónán reached up and plucked a long, red hair from his head. Together, they threaded the needle

Gently, they brought the glistening tip of the needle to the edge of the gash in Abel's neck. Rónán heard a light, melodic whispering that sounded like it came from his own lips. Rónán watched as his hand, interlaced with his mother's, drew intricate, delicate Ogham stitches through Abel's skin, closing the wound that had drained him of life. He plucked another hair from his head. Together he and his mother repeated their work, reattaching each finger, sewing it onto the stumps on Abel's hand.

This wasn't his mother working through him, but rather, her guidance, another lesson. While he felt her touch and hummed in harmony with her singing, Rónán felt in complete control of his actions. Hundreds of years of love and family history poured through and out him as he used his gift.

When each seam was carefully knotted and trimmed, Rónán leaned close to his friend's forehead. As he did so, he felt his mother slowly back away from him. Rónán whispered another prayer, putting every part of himself into his incantation. He heard the water behind him break, as if someone were stepping through the surface. He lightly kissed Abel's forehead and swiped his thumb gently across Abel's brow. A soft plop sounded behind him and then the pond stilled.

Rónán knew his mother was gone, though he could still feel her presence. He grasped Abel's hands in his own, kissing each palm gently. He closed his eyes, feeling the warmth of the sun and hearing the call of the birdsong overhead.

Rónán heard a loud gasp, as if someone had just crested through the water after desperately swimming for hours.

"Rónán?" he heard a dry, hoarse whisper.

Rónán's eyes shot open, and he looked at Abel's face. There, staring back at him, were the warm, honey brown eyes of his friend.

Rónán tried to speak, to say something, anything to Abel, but before he could, Abel pulled him into an embrace. Against Abel's bare chest, Rónán could feel their hearts beating quickly and forcefully and he was sure their chests rose and fell as one. A radiant heat spread between them, blanketing them both in a warmth greater than that of the sun above them.

"Abel, I—" Rónán began. But before he could finish his thought, Abel tucked a hand into Rónán's long hair and brought their lips together in a kiss.

When their lips touched, a tidal wave of joy washed over Rónán. He stayed afloat by holding onto Abel. They sat in their oasis beside the pond in the sun, embracing as if nothing else in the world mattered.

Chapter 14

"What happened?" Abel asked later, his voice still dry and hoarse. He reached up and fingered the stitches tenderly embroidered into his neck. "How am I here?"

Rónán decided to tell him the truth. He held Abel's uninjured hand as he recounted the events of the past day and a half. As Rónán spoke, Abel slowly flexed his fingers that had just moments ago been severed from his body. Hearing himself recite the details, Rónán thought they sounded ludicrous, like some macabre fairytale, but if Abel didn't believe him, he didn't show it.

"Wait, so your momma was the bride?" He asked intently. "And what did you tell Henriette? And Helene?"

Rónán felt another pang of guilt picturing the women in his head. "She was, and I didn't...I don't know..." his words trailed off. He tilted his head back, looking toward the sun, trying with everything to hold the tears in.

Abel brought his injured hand to Rónán's cheek, and Rónán felt the rough seams sewn around Abel's fingers.

"Hey. Don't worry about that now." Abel crooned. "We can figure it out later."

Rónán closed his eyes and leaned into Abel's hand. Gently, he kissed his fingers. They sat in silence for a moment, soaking up the sun, listening to the sounds of the wildlife around them. Rónán heard Abel release a loud, raspy sigh.

"We have to go back to Bridewater," Abel said, a darkness in his gravelly voice. "I have to talk to Douglas."

"Douglas?" Rónán interjected. "Abel, I don't know if–"

"I have to. He can't get away with what he did to me."

Rónán thought about what he wanted to say. "Abel, I—" but he was interrupted again.

"No. Douglas can't keep getting away with hurtin' people." He looked Rónán right in the eyes. "He killed me, Rónán. I'd still be dead if it wasn't for you. I must confront him, stop him from hurtin' anyone else. I have to help Clementine."

Rónán held his gaze. "And then what?" he asked, pleading in his voice. "*I'm* a killer, Abel."

Abel looked away before speaking. "Then, we'll leave. Get out of Bridewater."

As if a cloud had passed over them, fear shrouded Rónán. Get out of Bridewater? He had thought about it, of course, but where could they go? This town is the only thing Rónán had ever known, the shop his only home.

"This place, these people, are cursed and it has nothing to do with the bride," Abel said. "I'll tell Douglas I'm leavin', and we'll go. We'll just start walkin' and figure it out as we go."

Rónán nodded. He knew in his heart that he wasn't meant to stay in Bridewater forever. How could he continue to live in the place where his mother was taken from him and where he took Helene's father and Henriette's husband from them?

"Okay," he said. "We'll leave."

Abel kissed Rónán on the cheek. They unraveled their arms from one another. He stood and gingerly pulled on his clothes. After he was dressed, the boys leaned on each other and limped their way back toward Bridewater. Twilight was falling by the time they reached the town, so not much life was stirring, which they were both grateful for. They paused outside the tailor shop. They had agreed to part ways, allowing Rónán to pack some things while Abel spoke with Douglas alone, although the thought terrified Ronan.

Abel squeezed Ronan's hands and smiled., "I'll see you soon, *little seal.*"

Rónán entered his shop, the silvery bell announcing his arrival. The space that he had lived in for the last nineteen years suddenly seemed so large. He didn't know where to begin packing. He knew he couldn't take much, not that he had much to take, but every scrap of fabric and discarded thread had a memory attached to it. He retrieved his gunny sack and thought for a moment. He laid his mother's leather books into the bag, each one containing her lessons and drawings. He added a few vials, some of which still contained their home brews, wrapping them in a discarded piece of fabric to be sure they wouldn't break. He replenished his leather sewing pouch with sewing supplies, and placed it in the bag, as well. After all, what kind of tailor would he be without a needle and thread?

Padding up to his bedroom, Rónán looked around. He gently lowered his mother's diary into the bag, as if it were something precious and breakable. He folded his tree-embroidered bedroom curtains and added them, as well—one of the last projects he worked on with his mother. He picked up the violin case by the handle, knowing that he could not leave it behind because it was important to both of them.

Striding across the room, Rónán sat for the last time on the small stool in front of his mother's vanity. He ran a hand over the soft applewood desk, feeling each notch and groove of his father's handiwork. He looked at himself in the mirror, barely recognizable between the ripped stitches and discolored bruises. Looking at his face, he saw his mother reflected back at him. Despite the pain still radiating in his body, he smiled. He reached out both hands to grip the back of the ornamental mirror on either side and with a grunt of effort, ripped it from the two pieces of wood that held it over the vanity. It might be an impractical choice for their journey, but he couldn't leave it behind.

When Rónán was satisfied, he strode back down to the shop. Standing at the back door, he looked over his shoulder one last time to take in his home. With a sigh, he pulled open the painted green door and stepped out into the humid air. He peered up and down the alley. The only signs of movement were from the chickens lazily chattering in their enclosure behind the butcher shop. Rónán sat on the back steps, feeling his joints protest as he lowered himself. Suddenly exhausted, he placed his elbows on his knees and buried his head in his hands as he waited for Abel to return.

As he sat there, his head bowed, trying to make sense of everything, he heard a soft, lowing rumble. A slight pressure against his ankle made him lift his head and open his eyes. The orange tabby cat was weaving in and around his legs, purring, and occasionally throwing its head up toward Rónán. Rónán reached down and scratched the cat under its chin. The little tom stretched its neck out, its purrs growing louder. After a moment, the cat plopped itself onto its side and rolled onto its back, exposing its belly, looking up at Rónán expectantly. Rónán scratched the soft, white underbelly of the cat, and immediately its teeth grasped his arm and it playfully kicked at Rónán's wrists. Rónán laughed, watching the cat's tail as it darted back and forth.

A sudden, loud crashing noise made the cat jump up and sprint off down the alleyway. Rónán looked around, trying to identify the source of the noise. He heard what sounded like a struggle from a few doors down, and amidst the crashes were muffled, yet bellowing yells. With a jolt, he realized the noise was coming from the Duvall Family Butchery shop.

Rónán shot up and ran to the back door of the shop. "Abel?" he screamed inside to no answer.

The clattering sounds on the other side of the door were louder now. Rónán pounded his fist on the door, each beat sending a pulse of pain from his hand to his shoulder.

"Abel? Douglas? Open the door!"

The sounds grew more frantic on the other side of the door. The two men seemed to be roaring at one another, but Rónán could not make out what they were saying through the heavy wood. Rónán only knew he needed to get inside. He began heaving his shoulder into the door close to the knob that held it closed, his whole body screaming in pain with each contact of flesh on wood.

The door splintered and flew open, and Rónán tumbled to the floor of the butcher shop. His nostrils were filled with the coppery smell of blood mixed with a drunken odor of whiskey. Douglas and Abel were locked together, each one punching the other with any opening. A cut above Abel's eye gushed blood giving the impression of a kind of crude war paint.

"You were dead!" Douglas spat at Abel, "You're some kind of demon!" Something in Douglas' face looked unstable, like an unbelieving fear mixed with an unyielding anger. As he shouted, Douglas punched Abel in the gut, sending him sprawling to the floor, doubled over like he might vomit. Abel spit onto the floor, a tooth shooting from his mouth in a thick glob of viscous blood. He was on all fours, breathing heavy; tears of pain streaked down his face, drawing lines through the fresh, bright red blood on his cheeks.

Rónán took in the sight of Douglas' face. His lip had been split open and was swollen. A bright red and purple bruise puffed under his eye from where Abel's fist connected. His drunkenness painted his complexion in a mottled, ruddy pink, blending in with the bruises rising on his cheeks.

"I'll kill you again, you fucking demon," Douglas slurred. He stood over Abel, drawing back one of his legs. Rónán ran to him, tried to stop him, but a sickening thump told him that Douglas' boot connected with Abel's temple.

Abel's head flew to the side, twisting violently at the neck. He groaned and his breathing became heavier, more forced, and his eyes remained closed. Douglas took another drunken step towards his brother. He raised his boot again, aiming it down on Abel's head, but before he could, Rónán sprinted across the room and tackled him. Despite Douglas' larger size, he toppled to the ground in a pile with Rónán.

Rónán wanted to hurt him to return tenfold all the pain Douglas had given, but even in his drunkenness, Douglas' weight gave him an advantage. He quickly threw Rónán off of him. Grunting, he pushed himself back up to standing. He took heavy steps towards Rónán and gripped one hand behind his head, pulling his hair into a knot in his large fist. Douglas yanked, forcing Rónán to rise to a kneeling position, pulling his hair so hard that Rónán's head was forced upward, leaving his neck exposed. Rónán's eyes watered with pain.

"You," Douglas huffed coldly, "What did I tell you?" Douglas spat on the ground next to Rónán.

Douglas reached behind himself toward the counter as Rónán wriggled in his grip like a caught fish hanging from a line–the fisherman's prize catch. He looked at Rónán, and with each word punctuated by an earthy cloud of whiskey on his breath, Douglas shouted, "Leave my brother be."

Rónán felt a white hot, searing pain. With the last word he roared, Douglas shoved a boning knife into the meat between Rónán's chest and shoulder. Douglas let go of Rónán's hair, sending him crumpling to the floor, blood blooming like a perverse flower on his shirt from where the knife still lodged in his skin. Rónán looked at Abel who seemed to be struggling to stay conscious, his breaths more ragged and pained than they were a moment ago. He felt his own consciousness fading, and all he could think about was how sorry he was—sorry he had brought Abel into this situation, sorry for any pain he caused, and sorry that he and Abel would now die. There was nothing to do now but accept their shared fate.

Douglas took another long swig of whiskey, sending himself into a coughing fit. He swayed closer to Rónán and knelt on the ground next to him. He spoke again, his voice a mix of anger and sadness, "I told you to leave him alone."

Douglas wrapped his hands around Rónán's neck, trying to crush his windpipe with brute force. Rónán tried to breathe in but couldn't. His vision faded, as he choked, trying to hold onto consciousness. Finally, despite the pain, he was washed in a sense of peace. He knew he had reached his end, thinking that at least his pain would be over soon. He only hoped the same for Abel.

A wet *thunk* sounded in the room, and Rónán thought for a moment that maybe the bones in his neck had finally given way to Douglas' hands. But he felt Douglas' grip loosen. As the color came back to his vision, Rónán looked up, saw a new flicker of emotion in Douglas' eyes. Somewhere behind the sadness and the anger was something new. Fear.

A trickle of hot, red blood ran down the center of Douglas' face, cascading and dripping down the end of his nose. Rónán followed the trail upwards and saw a cleaver sticking out of Douglas' skull, slicing into bone and brain. His vision continued following the angle of the knife until he saw the slender hand that was wielding it belonged to none other than Clementine.

Chapter 15

Clementine's eyes were wide with horror, as if shocked to see the knife at the end of her own shaking arm. Her pale face was speckled with the butcher's blood, giving the impression that she somehow sprouted freckles to rival Rónán's own. For a moment, Rónán thought she might speak. Her lips parted, but no sound came out.

Rónán gripped the handle of the boning knife still sprouting from his body. With one swift movement, he unsheathed it from the muscle in his shoulder. His whole body began throbbing, but with all the strength he could muster, Rónán pulled himself over to where Abel lay unconscious.

"Abel?" Rónán pleaded, the sound coming out in a gurgle of blood.

The movement beneath Abel's eyelids told Rónán that he was still alive, but it was clear that he was hurting. Golden strands of hair were matted to his face with blood and deep purple bruises were like patches of wildflowers on his skin.

With an effort that sent radiating shockwaves up and down his spine, Rónán raised himself up to kneel next to Abel. He gently cradled the other boy's face in hands, as if he were holding a precious, breakable family heirloom. When Abel's face didn't shatter in his hands, Rónán tried saying his name again.

Abel's eyes flickered open momentarily, fluttering like the wings of a butterfly. After a moment, he was able to hold them open. Rónán was relieved to see Abel's golden-brown eyes staring back at him.

"*Little seal,*" Abel laughed, the movement of which made him wince in pain.

Through his tears, Rónán smiled back at Abel, and, not caring that Clementine still stood nearby, kissed him on the cheek leaving an imprint of his lips in the fresh blood.

Abel looked at Rónán, barely recognizable with the bright streaks of red lining his pale white face. His eyes took in the room. Broken and shattered remnants of his fight with Douglas littered the space around them. It was only now that he saw the knife splitting his brother's skull.

"Douglas," his eyes widened, "What…what happened?"

Finally free from her shock, Clementine released the handle of the cleaver. As if that were the only thing keeping Douglas upright, his body lurched forward. As he fell, a gurgling sound parted his lips, and he hit the floor with a wet thud. A long, low exhale signaled to the room that he would not be hurting anyone any longer.

Clementine brought her hands to her mouth and knelt to the ground next to her dead husband. Her slender frame was somehow made smaller by the mound of the large man on the ground in front of her.

"Douglas?" she said, whimpering. "Douglas, I'm sorry." She shook his shoulder. As if the full weight of her actions finally hit her, Clementine threw herself atop her husband's body and sobbed.

"Clem," Abel said gently. "You… you had to." With the help of Rónán, he pushed himself up to a seated position. Abel stretched his hand toward Clementine, wanting to comfort her, make her understand that everything was going to be okay.

"Clem, if you hadn't…" The words got caught in Abel's throat. Both he and Rónán would be dead without her, without the slick blade that severed Douglas' consciousness from his body.

Clementine didn't seem to hear. Her small frame shook with grief as she laid her forehead against Douglas' back. Rónán and Abel sat in silence now, with only the sounds of Clementine's heaving sobs and the rhythmic dripping of blood from Douglas' wound filling the space between them.

As Rónán looked at Clementine, he couldn't help but feel for her. He felt pity—pity for the woman who lived under the abuse of the men of Bridewater, the people who treated her like an object. Perhaps her decision was made out of love, to save the lives of the boys before her, but perhaps, some part of it was to save herself. No matter why, she decided to stop Douglas. Rónán could see that the emotions of that decision were eating at her now.

"Clem," Abel tried to address her. He again reached his hand toward her.

Clementine looked up, taking in the sight of the two bloodied and bruised young men in front of her, and something shifted in her face. The sadness was replaced by something else. In an instant, she squeezed her face together, like swallowing something sour.

"Leave," she said to the boys, in a short, clipped tone.

"Clementine," Abel repeated.

"LEAVE!" This time, she yelled it in their faces, holding the word out like the last note of a practiced aria.

Rónán stood, sending pins and needles through his joints. He looked down at Abel, offering a hand. As he struggled to his feet, Rónán ducked under his armpit to help him stand.

Clementine was now on her feet, too. In her determination, she seemed to grow in stature, driven by something instinctual. She reached across the countertop toward the bottle of whiskey and took a swig. The taste made her face contort, and she wiped her mouth with the back of her sleeve.

Clementine stepped lightly toward the boys, leaning in to kiss Abel on the cheek. "Leave," she repeated to them, but there was something different in her tone, something gentle. It wasn't a command; it was a plea.

Rónán and Abel watched as Clementine emptied the bottle of whiskey over Douglas. She then walked around the Duvall Family Butchery, emptying bottle after bottle, soaking the wooden walls and floorboards with spirits.

"Please, go," she pleaded again softly, with a sad acceptance in her eyes.

The boys strode from the shop, Rónán half carrying Abel through the back door to the alleyway beyond.

"Is she going to be okay?" Rónán asked Abel, glancing over his shoulder, hearing the sounds of more bottles breaking through the door.

"I'm not sure," Abel replied, a distant sadness in his expression. "What now?"

Rónán considered him for a second and remembered the boat he had left hidden in the reeds near the chapel. The two boys limped toward the tailor shop. After confirming Abel could stand and move on his own, Rónán grabbed his things—the bag, the fiddle, and the mirror. With them tucked under his arms, they began walking toward the wooden rowboat.

The night in Bridewater seemed to buzz with life though only Rónán and Abel were on the road. It was dark, but a gusty wind had picked up at some point in the evening, amplifying the sounds of the bay. When they reached the boat, Rónán lowered his belongings inside and helped Abel into the low seat. When Rónán began to walk into the water, he heard behind him a high-pitched, mewing sound.

Rónán turned to see the orange cat trotting to him along the waterline. When the tomcat reached him, it sat, staring at him with its golden eyes and tail hanging limp but alert, like a question mark.

"Hold on," Rónán said to Abel. He walked over to the cat and scooped it up. "Should we take him?" Rónán asked Abel.

Abel laughed, "I think we could use a friend."

Rónán handed the cat to Abel, and it immediately curled up at his feet in the boat. Wading up to his knees, he loosed the tethers of the boat and began pushing it out into the bay. When they were far enough into the water that he was confident it would hold them all up, Rónán jumped in next to Abel.

Rónán paddled them out. The waters were rough, but the boat seemed immune to the tossing waves. After a moment, he reached into his bag, pulling out the embroidered curtains from his bedroom. He quickly bundled them into a makeshift bed for the cat, placing them along the bottom of the boat. The cat sniffed his offering for a moment before lazily plopping himself into their folds. Rónán reached back into the bag to retrieve one of the many vials he packed before leaving his home. Inside was a minty, medicinal smelling liquid. He began to treat both his and Abel's wounds, alternately washing them with sea water and cleansing them with his mother's tincture.

"What is that?" Abel asked, breaking the silence between them.

Rónán turned, looking toward where Abel pointed. A faint orange glow softened the edges of darkness that blanketed the night. It almost looked as if the sun were rising.

"It can't be morning already," Abel thought aloud.

They watched for a few more moments, and the realization that the sun would rise behind them, not in front of them, dawned on Rónán.

"Abel, that's Bridewater," Rónán said softly. "It's… on fire."

Abel craned his neck to see better. The row of shops that faced the bay, including both the Duvall Family Butchery shop and Rónán's tailor shop, were burning. Even in the darkness, they could just see the thick gray plume rising above the row of shops. Rónán suspected the spark began in the butcher shop and then, carried by the heavy winds or someone's will, it traveled through Mr. Francis' offices and to the tailor shop. Even the years of humidity soaked into the very walls of the shops were not enough to stop the blaze.

Abel put his hand on Rónán's back. They watched as years of memories went up in smoke and down in ash. They weren't sure whether to laugh or to cry. They could just barely hear faint yells traveling over the waters, no doubt the men of Bridewater doing what they could to extinguish the flames, but Rónán couldn't help but feel like their efforts were in vain.

Rónán turned to Abel, "What now?" he asked.

Abel gave Rónán a smirk and shrugged. "I guess, we row," he said.

Rónán picked up the oars again and started paddling. He was moving them farther away from Bridewater, staying parallel to the coast. Rónán didn't know where they were going, but he figured they would know when they arrived. He looked toward Bridewater one last time. Even at this distance, the flames were still visible. At this angle, the black silhouette of the Baptist chapel stood out, illuminated from behind by the orange glow of the flames consuming Bridewater. There was something ominous but final about this sight, like cutting the final thread on a finished seam.

Taking his gaze away from the flames, he looked back at Abel. Somehow, even across the waters, Abel's golden-brown eyes seemed to reflect the soft glow of the flames. Rónán smiled. The hummingbird in his chest seemed to spring to life again, but this time, it wasn't trying to leave him.

*   *   *

Far into the sea beyond their boat, a head surfaced from the water. Aislyn looked proudly toward her son. She thought for a moment about the visions she had divined years ago as a new mother, and now, she knew her visions to be true. Rónán was made for something important. She knew in her heart that he would be okay; he would be safe. With one last smile toward the boat paddling off into the horizon, Aislyn fell back into the waters, sinking to eternity.

About the Author

C.R. Fagan is an author from the southern U.S. who primarily writes queer, historical fiction, much of which is infused with magic and folklore. Beyond writing, he works as a university educator. When not drafting his next work in progress or teaching on campus, he can be found spending time with his partner and his pets.

Acknowledgements

I have so many people to thank.

To my friends Genesis and Duck who heard the first whispers of this story years before a single word was written down, thank you for pushing me to finally take the leap to put words to paper. And thank you to Duck for taking Rónán from my mind's eye to the page with the first character art.

To my beta readers—Hannah, Jackie, Jamie, Kayla, and Kyle—thank you for spending so much time with what was definitely a mess of a draft. Your feedback helped bring the story to life.

To the Blue Cedar Press team—Gretchen, Laura, and Mike—thank you for taking a chance on me and allowing me to share Rónán's story.

To my family, thank you for supporting me no matter what ideas I pursue. It was your stories of my great grandmother's Irish heritage—specifically the imagery of her bonnet—that inspired Aislyn. I wanted to know more about where she came from, and I wove what I learned throughout this story.

To my partner. I will always be amazed how you listen to every story I share and how I feverishly tell you about my next character, no matter how underdeveloped at the time. Thank you for always being my cheerleader. I love you.

Finally, to my readers, you help make this dream of mine possible. Thank you for spending time in the swamps with Rónán and Abel. I hope you come back to them during their next adventure.

C.R. Fagan
September 2025